Hot Mess

Hot Mess

A Hot Aussie Knights Romance

Amy Andrews

TULE
PUBLISHING

Hot Mess

Tule Publishing First Printing, June 2017

The Tule Publishing Group, LLC

ISBN: 978-1-946772-75-6

Dedication

To Sinclair, Victoria and Trish. For the laughs, the stories and the pics of sooty firemen stripping off after a long hot day. Let's do it again sometime! And to Brooke Dell-Sewell for her help with the lawyer bits – couldn't have done it without her!

Prologue

THE CATHEDRAL WAS packed. Standing room only at the back, the mourners spilling out onto the wide, stone steps at the cathedral's entrance and through its ornate side doors.

Leonard Knight would have hated it.

The old man hadn't believed in pomp and ceremony. Or being the centre of attention. He'd believed in God and family and getting the job done – quietly, efficiently, and effectively.

He'd believed in hard work, in strategy, and he'd believed in his men.

Men who were, today, honouring him with the highest accolade that could be bestowed upon a fallen fire fighter of such distinction. A funeral with full honours for the man who was a legend in the ranks of Australian fire fighters.

The fire service was burying one of their own – their commissioner no less – and they could out pomp a royal wedding.

Rows and rows of bright-buttoned, shiny-shoed, uniformed men and women filled the pews of the cathedral, sitting stiffly erect, their dress hats on their laps.

Logan Knight was one of them but he had a front seat view.

He stuck his finger inside his collar and eased it off his neck for what felt like the hundredth time. It was a scorching January day outside and warmer still inside the packed cathedral. Plus, he was as uncomfortable wearing his formal uniform as his grandfather had been.

He hadn't joined the fire department to don a suit and tie. Neither had Leonard; although, he'd spent the last decade of his life doing just that.

Logan's gaze fixed on his grandfather's polished cherry-wood coffin, the brass trimmings shining as brightly as the buttons on Logan's uniform. It was draped in the fire services flag and topped with enough flowers to open a garden shop. It was hard to believe that a wooden box – no matter how fancy – could hold the man who had always been larger than life.

He stuck his finger into his collar again.

"Stop fidgeting, for fuck's sake," his cousin Caleb muttered beside him as some dignitary droned on at the lectern. "You're worse than a two-year-old with worms."

"He'd have hated this," Logan muttered back out the corner of his mouth.

"I know."

"Funerals are for the living, not the dead," chimed in

Dylan, Caleb's twin brother, from the other side.

Logan ran a belligerent eye over his cousin. "Thank you, Socrates."

The sound of muted sobbing filled the sudden silence as the dignitary finished up and Logan glanced over to the row of pews to his right to see his father and Dylan and Caleb's father comforting their mother. His other uncles – Leonard had seven sons – looked everything from stoic and stiff-upper-lipped to haggard. They all sat in the first row with their mother, their formal uniforms neat as pins, shouldering her through the shock of the sudden and unexpected death of her beloved husband of fifty years.

Logan had never seen his grandmother cry before – not once – and it pulled at his gut to see it now.

"Let us pray," the minister announced from the pulpit indicating that everyone should rise.

"Christ," Dylan muttered quietly as the congregation rose. "I could murder a beer."

Logan bit the inside of his lip to stop from laughing. It was one of their grandfather's favourite expressions.

"There'll be plenty of that at the wake," Logan murmured as he bowed his head. "Now shut up or Caleb'll give you a wedgie."

The minister's, "Dear Lord," drowned out the muffled chuckles from the Knight boys.

SEVERAL HOURS LATER, jackets discarded, ties loosened, sleeves rolled up, the cousins were on their fourth round of Rosie's house beer. Rosie's was an institution to Brisbane firefighters; a bar that had welcomed the city's finest for over thirty years. Leonard Knight had spent a lot of hours after knock-off with his mates here back in the early days of his career.

Just two blocks from Logan's station house, Rosie's had closed its doors this afternoon to everyone but emergency services personnel as it, too, paid tribute to Leonard's legacy.

And it was wall-to-wall uniforms.

Logan glanced around. It seemed like he was related to half the people in the room. His father and his uncles were scattered around, reminiscing about their old man, his three brothers were also drinking in a big group, all laughing loudly about some anecdote or other. Not to mention the thirty or forty cousins and seconds cousins and variety of prick relations—as his grandfather so colourfully called them—dotting the bar area.

Many of them had flown from interstate to attend. Caleb and Dylan had come from Adelaide. Even his cousin, Dare Knight, a smoke jumper from Montana, had flown in from the States.

The Knights were about as much of an institution in firefighting circles as Rosie's was.

"To the old man," Dare said. Her American twang seemed even more accentuated surrounded as she was by a bunch of macho Aussie blokes.

She hadn't seen her grandfather, or any of them except Logan, since her family's last visit to Australia when she'd been fifteen, but her grief was as tangible as theirs. Thankfully she was staying on at his firehouse for a while as part of an exchange programme. Logan had done the same thing a few years back, joining Dare's firehouse in Montana for a couple of years and he was looking forward to reconnecting with his kickass, GI Jane cousin.

Although, there was something new and edgy about her that worried him. Something that lay buried beneath the big smile and the electric blue dress that was turning heads left and right.

They drank to Leonard as they had the last three times. Normally, when Knight cousins got together, they smack talked relentlessly but the mood was distinctly sombre today.

"Do you think it was the investigation that killed him?"

Dare asked the question that had been bugging Logan since the news of their grandfather's death broke a week ago.

She might live on the other side of the world but the Knight clan was tight and she knew all about the investigation into the multi-departmental mismanagement that had led to the disastrous outcomes from the massive bush fire that had ravaged vast tracts of land down south a few months ago.

One hundred and eight people dead, three of them firefighters. He and Caleb and Dylan had been there, along with half the guys in the room, travelling to help their interstate brothers fight the firestorm side-by-side.

The loss of life – particularly his comrades – had gutted Leonard. Then the blame game had started. The government was looking for a scapegoat to divert attention from decades of funding cuts.

"He *was* seventy," Caleb said.

"Yeh, but he was fitter than a lot of men half his age," Dylan countered.

"Apparently not," Caleb shot back.

The twins glared at each other over their beers. Strikingly similar, they were both tall and broad and blond, which killed with the ladies. They played on their similarities too, often pretending to be the other to keep the women guessing.

Of course, their attitudes gave them away quickly. Dylan was relentlessly upbeat but Caleb, since his divorce, had turned into a cynic. His ex had accused him of being married to the job and hell if that wasn't true.

Half the guys in this joint were divorced because fighting fires was like some kind of drug. It could be hard for partners to understand. God knew, the only woman who'd ever managed to capture Logan's heart had struggled with it too. At the end anyway.

"What happened with those fires was not his fault," Logan said, breaking the tension between the brothers stirred up by grief and booze.

"You think that matters?" Caleb snorted. "Shit moves uphill; you know that. The guy at the top always carries the can. That's why they get paid the big bucks."

"That's crap," Dylan said. "Those fires were a cock up because of chronic underfunding and mismanagement at the local and state levels."

No one who had been on the ground had doubted that. It had been shocking. Logan had seen things he hadn't seen during his nine years on the job. Things he couldn't unsee. Things that still sometimes woke him in the middle of the night.

Property, livestock, people.

And his grandfather, who had felt every one of those deaths personally, had been hung out to dry. No wonder the old man's heart had given way after fifty years of dedicated service to the job.

Caleb snorted. "You think the politicians give a shit about the facts? And now he's gone that makes him an even easier target."

Logan suspected Caleb was right but he didn't want to think about it today. Today, they were supposed to be celebrating their grandfather's life, not talking politics either national or departmental.

He was pretty sure Leonard Knight would kick their asses for not already being drunk and talking football and women.

"Dude." Dare shook her head at Caleb then took a deep

swallow of her cold beer. "You need to get laid."

The change of subject worked as the guys laughed. "Just because I'm divorced doesn't mean I'm not getting any."

Logan kicked up an eyebrow. "Are you doing it wrong? 'Cause Dare's got a point, man. You are a little uptight. I could give you some pointers if you like."

"Hey, if he wants pointers, he doesn't have to go any further than his own brother." Dylan puffed out his chest. "The ladies love them some of this."

Caleb shook his head in disgust. "Get your hand off it."

Logan laughed and raised his glass. "To getting laid and fighting fires."

Glasses clinked and they drank. Then they drank some more. Then they all went and got tattoos…

Chapter One

LOGAN KNIGHT STOOD at the upstairs windows of the firehouse with his brother Duncan indulging in one of their favourite pastimes – guess the panties. So far they'd spotted several thongs, a lot of bikini briefs and the odd pair of grundies—granny undies.

One of the advantages of the house being in the centre of Brisbane was its proximity to the large population of female workers. It didn't hurt that it was smack bang in the middle of a street strewn with cafes and bars ensuring that a good proportion of these women walked past the house during their lunch breaks.

"I reckon that one's going completely commando," Duncan said, pointing to a redhead with no discernible panty line. Or DPL as they liked to call it.

"Hard to tell in jeans," Logan mused. "Could be a thong. She'd have to bend over to be sure. I need to see lack of butt floss."

And then, as if by magic, the woman dropped something and folded over from the waist as she snatched it off the ground.

"Well, whaddya know?" Duncan grinned. "There *is* a god."

"Awesome mind control, Bro." Logan high-fived his brother as they watched the low-riding jeans do their thing, sliding perilously lower. No peek of the thin elastic straps of a thong which would definitely be on display by now had she been wearing one.

"Damn, man, I think you're right. She's not wearing any panties."

"You two are deviants."

Logan grinned at Duncan as they turned to face their colleague.

"Sure," Duncan agreed, unperturbed by the characterisation. "But we're loveable deviants, right?"

Ruth Gilligan stood, arms crossed, shaking her head at them. At twenty-nine, the same age as Logan, she was one of only two women that made up the thirty-strong squad. And the only black female firefighter in the state.

Originally from one of the smaller islands in the Torres Strait, she was fit and strong and excellent at her job. She wasn't afraid of hard work, pulled her weight, and didn't take any of their shit. She could shoulder lift a hundred and fifty kilo man as easily as she could put him on his ass if he gave her any lip.

"I think that's an oxymoron," she said.

"Aww, come on now, Gilligan, that's no way to talk

about my baby brother." Duncan jabbed his fist at Logan's gut but he was way too fast for his older brother, laughing easily as he dodged the hit.

Ruth rolled her eyes. "I rest my case." She joined them at the window, perusing the parade of people out front. "Any decent guys out there? Someone who doesn't mind a strong, black woman with, according to my last boyfriend, a reckless death wish?"

"I hate to break this to you, Gilligan, but we haven't exactly been checking the dudes out. Besides…" Duncan thumped his chest. "Why look any further when you have such awesome specimens at your fingertips?"

"No thanks, I know where you dirty bastards have been." She pointed to a woman in a clingy T-shirt. "That chick's not wearing a bra."

Logan and Duncan's heads quickly snapped to the direction of Ruth's point. As a breast man, Logan enjoyed the bouncy view. It wasn't very PC but hell if he cared right at this moment.

"Looks like it's cold out as well," Duncan mused, a laugh in his voice.

It was hot enough to melt bitumen.

The woman turned into a building and disappeared and Logan glanced at Ruth. "I thought you were sworn off men. Or were waiting for Chris Hemsworth or something like –"

"Hey, dude," Duncan interrupted, "there's a woman looking up at the house who's the spitting image of Bella."

Bella? Logan's pulse spiked.

"What?" He whipped his head back to the street view, his gaze hunting up and down, searching for long blonde hair. "Where?" He growled, not seeing anyone who remotely matched her description.

Duncan pointed. "Sitting on that low wall over there under the tree. She's eating a sandwich or something."

Heartbeat stampeding like a herd of rhino through all his pulse points, Logan's gaze settled on the woman in question. His first thought was to reject his brother's assertion out of hand. Everything about her was just… different.

She was too far away to assess the colour of her eyes but this woman had short, choppy hair, more honey than blonde. There was more padding on her bones although, God knew, Bella had been too skinny. But more than that, it was the way she sat, the way she held herself.

She was too… tranquil. Relaxed. Serene. Or something…

Arabella Tucker had been a ball of energy. Sitting under a tree, unhurriedly eating as if she had all the time in the world had not been part of her repertoire. Released from the strictures of her good-girl upbringing when she'd been nineteen, she'd launched herself into life full steam ahead and he'd been hard put keeping up with her.

Sky diving. Bungee jumping. Rock climbing. White river rafting. Clubbing all night. Early morning jogging along the river banks or heading to the coast at dawn for a surf, the sun rising behind them as they rode their boards into the shore.

Being with her had been the most exhilarating – and gut-wrenching – year of his life.

Suddenly, the woman opposite tilted her head. That was all – just a slight movement really. But she might as well have stood up and slugged him with a blast from a fire hose for the impact the mannerism had on him. He sucked in a breath.

It *was* her. He'd know that head tilt anywhere. Arabella Tucker.

Bella.

His brother frowned. "Logan?"

"Christ," he said, pushing a hand through his short brown hair. "I think you're right."

Logan blinked. And blinked again. Why the hell was she just sitting there outside, studying the firehouse like a… architectural student – like a stranger – instead of a woman who knew it inside out?

Why hadn't she come in and asked for him? Sure, they hadn't parted ways on the best of terms but that was eight years ago for fuck's sake. Wasn't she at least curious about him? Didn't she want to at least say hi for old time's sake?

"What are you going to –"

Logan didn't give his brother a chance to finish. He didn't stop to consult or converse with either him or Ruth. He just ran. Ran like the city was burning down and only he could put it out.

She might not want to renew acquaintance but he sure as hell did. There was a part of him that always wondered about her. How she was doing? Where life had taken her? Was she a lawyer now? Had she married? Did she have children?

His lungs felt too big for his chest at the thought. Was she happy?

Now he had the chance to find out.

All three of the large, red station doors that had formed part of the iconic façade of the station since it had been built over a hundred years ago were open as his foot hit the cement of the engine bay. He scissor-jumped over a pile of equipment in his way. It was being sorted by one of the squad and Logan's jump almost put the guy on his ass.

"Fuck, man, where's the fire?"

Logan ignored him. He just kept going, his gaze eagerly searching for the woman as he burst onto the busy street. She had sunglasses on now and she was standing, crumpling up the sandwich wrapper in her hand and walking towards a nearby bin, still looking in his direction.

A steady stream of cars separated them and he waved at her as he waited impatiently for a break in the traffic. She didn't acknowledge him but who could tell where she was actually looking behind those dark lenses?

The lights at the intersection changed and Logan took advantage of the slowing traffic as she turned away. He weaved in between the cars, hitting the pavement at a half jog.

"Bella," he called to her back as she walked in the opposite direction.

She didn't stop. Or turn around. Maybe she hadn't heard him? He lengthened his stride, quickly closing the distance between them.

"Bella," he said again, reaching for her arm, sliding his hand onto it, pulling on it to slow her down.

She slowed, stopped, turned and glanced down at his hand before raising her face. The tint of her glasses made it impossible to see her eyes properly but she was definitely looking at him now.

"Bella." He smiled, the familiar feeling of *her* seeping through his gut.

She frowned at him and pulled her arm away.

"It's me," he said, his hand falling away. "Logan."

She stared at him for long moments, her head tilted just so again, her teeth sinking into her bottom lip the way they'd always done when she was contemplating something. "I see."

Logan blinked. *I see?* What the fuck did that mean? She was looking at him like she wasn't sure of him, like she didn't even *know* him. She might have wiped him all those years ago and she might not still feel the familiar flare sparking to life inside him all over again but she *had* felt it once upon a time.

As keenly, as desperately as him. Of that he *was* sure.

No way could eight years erase the memory of that. Hell, he doubted eighty years was enough.

She pulled off her sunglasses, the blue-green of her eyes as familiar to him as his own flinty grey. Her gaze roamed over his face, inspecting it, a slight frown drawing together honey-blonde eyebrows. "We… know each other, don't we?"

"Ha!" Logan laughed. "Very funny, Bella."

"Bella…"

She said it quietly, drawing the word out, as if she was weighing it up, testing it to see how it sounded on her tongue. Logan supposed back in snooty Melbourne with her snooty family in their snooty legal world she'd reverted to Arabella.

Christ, she looked good. Sure, she was looking wary and slightly puzzled but it was a vast improvement on the last time he'd seen her. Her face puffy and tear-stained, a blank, tired look staring back at him.

She looked healthy. Well.

The questions crowded his brain thick and fast until the pressure of them became too much and they were spilling out his mouth. "How… have you been? What are you doing in Brisbane? How long have you been here for? You cut your hair."

He brought his hand up to touch it but she tensed and he dropped it, his stomach dropping as well. He ploughed on trying to ignore the sick feeling in his gut. "Are you a lawyer now? Are you… here with anyone? Are you… married?"

A husband. God, even the thought of it burned like the

twist of a hot poker into his flesh. She wasn't wearing a ring. But that didn't necessarily mean anything. Because why wouldn't she be married? Why wouldn't some guy have snapped her up by now?

"No." She shook her head. "No husband."

Logan's breath rushed out on a relieved sigh. No husband. But there could still be a partner. There could be… kids.

"Look, I'm sorry." She reached for his hand and held it loosely. He battled the urge to hold tighter not wanting to freak her out. "I really have to get back to court but… there was an accident. A few years ago, I was hurt. I… lost my memory. I have amnesia."

Amnesia.

After, when Logan tried to recall this conversation, all he'd remember was the relentless beat of the sun on his shoulders and that word.

"Amnesia?"

She nodded quickly already shifting away from him. "Yes. I lost nine years. Everything from fifteen to twenty-four"—she used her hand to mimic an explosion coming from her head—"all gone. But I'm sorry…" She checked her watch and took a step back. "I really have to go. Maybe we could… meet for a coffee or a drink or something and I can explain more?"

Logan's brain was not functioning properly at all. *Bella had amnesia.* He'd met her when she'd been nineteen so that meant…

She didn't remember him.

Didn't remember kissing under the stars on a Croatian beach, didn't remember skinny-dipping with him at a secluded cove in the Whitsundays, didn't remember him proposing to her on top of the Story Bridge.

Didn't remember the baby.

"We don't have to," she said, her voice quiet, a frown knotting her brows as she took another step away from him.

Logan shook his head, dragging himself away from their memories and the devastating realisation that only *he* remembered them. "No… Yes…" He took a step towards her. "I'd like that." He had to know more. "What about after work this afternoon? I knock off at five?"

She nodded and relief flowed cool and swift through his veins. "I do too. Officially. But things often run later. Is six too late?"

"That should work for me. At Rosie's?"

She winged her eyebrows. "Rosie's?"

Christ. *She didn't remember Rosie's.* Didn't remember that mind-blowingly dirty quickie they'd had in the back alley late one night when neither had been able to wait long enough to get home.

"It's a pub," he said. "It's two blocks that way." He pointed in the opposite direction.

"Okay." She nodded. "I'll find it. I might be a bit late; sometimes court is like that."

"I'll wait."

"All right." She backed away another step. "See you then." And she turned on her heel and walked away.

Logan shoved his hand through his hair as he watched her retreating back, his brain officially blown. Her straight skirt pulled taut across her backside and he absently noted a slight unevenness to her gait at the same time he thought *bikini briefs.*

It was easier than trying to wrap his head around Bella's bombshell.

Amnesia?

Fuck.

Chapter Two

LOGAN'S GUT WAS still churning two hours later as he dialled the Melbourne number. As soon as he'd set foot back in the station they'd gone out to a job. A small grass fire on some vacant, inner-city land. It had kept his mind occupied for a while but done nothing for the steady churn in his gut.

When he'd returned to the station he'd Googled the fuck out of amnesia. And then he'd gone to the yellow pages online and looked up a number.

The beat of his heart echoed through his ears and his hands shook as he waited for the other end to pick up.

"Good afternoon. Tucker, Tucker, Granville, and Morgan, how may I direct you?"

Logan took a steadying breath. "I'd like to talk to Mr. Tucker, please." He hadn't been able to unearth a home phone number but the fancy-pants, Collins Street law firm founded by Arabella's grandfather was an easy find.

"Mr. Tucker Senior or Mr. Tucker Junior?"

Logan stomped down his impatience and the growing

anger. Why the fuck hadn't her parents told him? "Senior." It was terse but he didn't care.

"Hold, please, while I check if he's available. Who may I say is calling?"

His knuckles tightened around the phone. The chirpiness of the receptionist was getting on Logan's last nerve and her fancy speak for Mr. Tucker decides who he did and didn't talk to pissed him off even more.

His blue-collar roots dug in a little deeper.

The truth was, he and Daddy Tucker had history. If he gave his real name, would the old man refuse to talk to him as he had in the past?

"Tell him it's about his daughter. About Bel…Arabella."

"Putting you through, hold please."

Logan took little comfort from her immediate response. Tucker Senior might refuse to talk to him but he'd always been very protective – *overly protective* – of his daughter and he must be crapping himself knowing she was far away from him again and in Logan's territory to boot.

Amnesia or no amnesia.

Amnesia… Fuck. Didn't that only happen to people in the movies? His Internet search had left him even more confused and not at all comforted that Bella would suddenly remember him just because they'd become reacquainted.

Their meeting might have been serendipitous but where they went to from here, he had no idea.

Who knew serendipity could be such a bitch?

"Hello? Who the hell is this?"

The old man's bluster hadn't changed in eight years. The pompous tone of his Toorak upbringing still grated. "It's Logan."

There was a pause. A very long pause. Followed by an audible sigh. "Logan."

"Surprise." It gave him no pleasure to have discomforted the man. Not like Logan had imagined it might.

"You've seen her?"

"Today. She was outside the firehouse looking up at it as if she'd never seen it before. Imagine my surprise to find out it was because she doesn't *remember* having ever seen it."

There was more silence on the line. But it was heavy. Weighted. As if the old man was trying to figure out a way forward. Or another way to screw Logan over.

"Why didn't you tell me she'd been in an accident?"

"Logan…" Another sigh. "You hadn't been together for almost five years when she had the accident." The old man's tone was conciliatory. He sounded weary which wasn't something Logan had ever associated with Bella's father.

"I still would have come."

"Yes." It was a simple acknowledgement that spoke volumes.

Graham Tucker, it seemed, finally understood the depth of Logan's feelings for Bella. Which was precisely why they hadn't told him.

It was a vindication but an empty one and it needled.

"Well, screw you very much," Logan muttered on a well of anger and grief.

"Now listen, Son…"

The weariness in the old man's voice had evaporated and Logan could almost picture him stiffening in his expensive leather Chesterfield desk chair.

"If you think we had the time or mental capacity to worry about the wants and needs of a *boyfrien*d from five years prior then you're even more self-centred than I remember."

Boyfriend? *Boyfriend*? "I wasn't just her boyfriend and you know it."

"Yes, Logan," he said in his best high-priced lawyer voice, "you were. You think we should have contacted all her exes and let them know she was in intensive care while we were desperately worried she was going to die?"

Logan ignored the *all her exes* quip, zeroing in on the intensive care bit. *Jesus.* The thought of it made him want to lose his lunch.

"It was bad."

A pause. "Yes."

The weariness was back but it was clear that Tucker Senior wasn't going to elaborate. Logan didn't force the issue. However bad it had been she'd clearly recovered – physically anyway – he could ask Bella the details in a couple of hours.

"She says she has amnesia."

"Yes."

"How bad is it?" Logan needed to know. She didn't remember anything, she'd said, but maybe that had been a sweeping statement for the purposes of brevity. She'd been in a hurry after all.

"She lost nine years of her life."

"*Everything?*"

"Yes Son. *Everything...*I'm sorry."

For what it was worth the old man actually sounded sorry but Logan didn't need or want his pity. He needed this not to be true. *He needed her to remember.* "Is it permanent? What do the doctors say?"

"Yes, it is. The doctors say it's highly unlikely that she'll ever get her memory back."

"Highly unlikely... But not impossible, right?" he pressed.

He'd read cases where amnesia sufferers got their memories back. They did in the movies all the time.

"Logan... the doctors say that if she'd been going to get any of it back it would have returned in those months following. It's been four years."

"But... I've read about it... seen stories on the news. It *does* happen."

"The doctors say those cases are rare and usually sensationalised. That memory return almost never happens. Her neurosurgeon has never seen one case."

Logan ran a hand over his head. Christ. This *could not* be happening. To have connected with Bella again only to discover she didn't know him from Adam was a particularly cruel twist of fate.

God *fucking* damn it.

"You didn't tell her about me?"

"No."

"Or the baby?"

"*No.*"

Logan had been prepared for the first answer but not the second. He sucked in a breath. The storm of feelings over the loss of their baby had lessened over the years but it squalled in his gut again, physical pain streaking through his veins like forks of lightning.

Pain magnified by knowing he was the sole keeper of those memories now. It was hard to fathom something that had been etched on their souls could ever be erased and he suddenly felt devastatingly alone.

"Don't you think she has a right to know?" he demanded, his voice a low growl as he leaned forward and shut the door of the small offices he was using. "That she was pregnant? That she gave birth to a baby even if that baby never drew a breath?"

"You think that was an easy decision to make? That we did it to *slight* you?" The old man was defensive now.

"Well, I don't know rightly what the fuck you were thinking," Logan snapped. "Other than perhaps being able to once and for all erase anything to do with me and her and the life we had together."

Silence once again. Long drawn out silence. And then

finally, "You don't understand."

Graham's defensiveness had dissipated but Logan wasn't in the mood to go easy. "Don't tell me I don't understand," he said, his voice icy. "I loved her too, damn it."

He sighed. "She was so… lost and sad and fragile after the baby."

"*I know*," Logan said testily.

"She fell into a terrible depression. Wouldn't eat properly, slept hardly at all, couldn't concentrate, couldn't …function I guess. Her mother and I despaired. It's a terrible thing to see your child go through something like that. If I could have reached inside her and taken away all that turmoil, I would have."

Logan shut his eyes against the pain gripping his heart. *He'd* wanted to be there. To love her through it. To help. He'd tried but she'd rejected him. Twice. Hadn't wanted him there.

Her parents hadn't either.

But, strangely enough, as Graham's anguish crackled down the line, Logan felt sorry for the old man. Logan didn't doubt him when he said he would have taken Bella's pain if it had been possible.

They might never have gotten on but Logan hadn't ever doubted how much her father loved her.

"Gradually, after about a year, with antidepressants and therapy she got better. She went back to law school, resumed her life. But she was never the same. Always just a little bit sad. The sparkle in her eyes was gone. We'd hear her crying at night sometimes and it broke out hearts. And then the accident happened and all we were worried about for so long was getting her through it. Taking a day at a time. Being there for her as she recovered from her head injury and through two years' rehab for her pelvic injuries."

"*Two years*? Christ." She must have been in a helluva mess.

"Yes. Indeed."

Logan thought he heard the echo of a smile in Tucker Senior's voice.

"We didn't make an active decision to *not* tell her about the baby, Logan," he continued. "We just kept putting it off, hoping she might get some or all of her memory back. But… she didn't. She was, however, a completely different person. She was the *old* Arabella. The fifteen-year-old. Happy and bright and positive. The sparkle was back in her eyes. She returned to the law firm as a paralegal, she made friends, she went out, her appetite was back. For so long, after the baby, we'd hoped and prayed that our old fun-loving Arabella would come back and suddenly she was. And I'm sorry but neither her mother nor I could bear making her relive that dark place all over again."

Logan squeezed his eyes shut, his throat thick with emotion, his nose prickling from the urgent press of tears behind his lids.

God fucking damn it.

This was so unfair. He'd be a right prick if he couldn't see Graham Tucker's side of things but… being erased like that? Everything they'd had just… gone?

Man, that shit *hurt*.

"You're seeing her again."

It wasn't a question. It was a statement. And a step up from the old man's previous imperious edicts forbidding Logan from having anything to do with Bella.

Logan opened his eyes. "Yes."

"Can you please just tread carefully with what you tell her?"

There wasn't one part of Logan that didn't want to tell Graham Tucker to go fuck himself. *He* wasn't the one she'd forgotten. But Logan had heard the real anguish in the old man's voice. This situation sucked for both of them. And he was a lot less hot headed than he'd been at twenty.

He sighed. "Does she know anything about the time she was here? Does she know she even lived here?"

"She knows she went on a Contiki tour and lived in Brisbane for a year when she was nineteen but only because we've told her and she's seen the photos from that time."

Photos? He knew those photos. Christ, he'd been in most of them. "So who the hell does she think the guy was who's all over her in those pictures?"

"*Those* ones were erased."

Logan's pulse spiked as his spare hand curled into a fist. "Are you shitting me? You even *erased* the photos?"

God, he felt like he was in the middle of a bad Cold War movie where all trace of him was being eradicated.

"No." Tucker Senior's denial was quick and emphatic. "She did, Logan. When she first came back to Melbourne after the baby."

The information hit him like a punch to the gut. *Bella had erased him…* Twice.

"Well… that worked out well for you, didn't it?"

He made no attempt to hide the bitterness in his voice. Rationally, he knew it wasn't the other man's fault but right in this moment he didn't care.

Jesus Christ, he was so fucking angry he wanted to tear the world down with his bare hands.

"I know you don't like me very much, Son –"

"For the love of God," Logan interrupted, his blood pressure rising as a flash of red sprayed across his vision like blood splatter, "quit calling me *Son*. I'm not your son and I'm not some twenty-year-old kid anymore either."

"Okay…" A pause. "Fair enough. Logan… I know you probably don't feel like doing me any favours, I know I made it difficult for you with Arabella but I'm begging you, from one man who loves her to another, please don't tell her about the baby."

Logan snorted. "I remember a time you would have begged me to stay the hell away from her."

"A lot's changed, Logan. I'm just grateful she's still alive. I'm not interested in controlling her life anymore."

"Except for not telling her about the baby."

"What on earth good will it do telling her, Logan?" he asked. "So you feel better? So *we* feel better? So our guilt is assuaged?" His questions were quiet but carried a hell of a lot of punch. Graham was calling Logan out on his selfishness. "Do I have your agreement?"

A sarcastic reply about signing a stat dec rose inside Logan, welling from the deep, bitter pit of his history with Bella's father. He forced it down. Now was not the time to be a smartass. Her father was asking a serious question.

One that not only took away a part of his history, a part of what had moulded him, but one that had consequences. One that made him feel exceedingly uneasy.

"Christ, Graham…"

Once upon a time, Logan had called him *Sir* because he'd been raised to respect his elders but right now they were just two men united in a moral dilemma together. Not in a million years would Logan have ever thought he'd be walking in Graham Tucker's shoes.

Nothing felt right about it. He understood the man's reasons, he understood the motivations, but it still felt wrong.

"Doesn't she need to know from a medical standpoint that she's been pregnant before? What if she wants to start a family? What if there're complications? She should have an accurate medical record, surely?"

Logan was trying to be practical. Trying to not let *his*

emotions muddy the waters. This wasn't about him being self-serving. It was just common sense.

"We'll cross that bridge if and when we get to it, I guess."

"Oh, yeah?" Logan snorted. "Was that your theory where her meeting up with me again was concerned? How'd that work out for you?"

"Not so well as it turned out," the older man admitted, his tone rueful. "I tried to talk her out of coming to Brisbane."

Yeah. *So much for not controlling her life anymore.*

"But then I discovered you were stationed out in Western Queensland somewhere and I thought… what were the chances?"

What were the chances indeed? If Logan had been a more spiritual dude he could have made a lot of the universe bringing him and Bella together *twice*. But he didn't believe in any of that bullshit so he focused on the more alarming revelation. "*Discovered?*"

"I made…"

The old man's voice drifted off and Logan imagined him waving an imperious hand in a dismissive *the rich shall inherit the earth* wave.

He should have been angry but it seemed like he was fresh out at the moment. There'd been too much anger and helplessness these last eight years.

"Discreet enquiries, shall we say?"

Logan ignored the irritating superiority of his admission. "I *have* been out west. I transferred back a few weeks ago."

He'd been notified of his successful application to go back to the house that had trained him two days before the news of his grandfather's death.

"You're in Brisbane for a while?"

"Yes. I'm not going anywhere."

He wasn't going to pussyfoot around with Bella's father this time. He had no idea what, if anything, might develop with them – at the moment he just needed to see her, to know for sure that he was lost to her.

"So…"

The question hung between them for a beat or two. Logan didn't need to ask him to elaborate. "I don't feel right about this."

"You think I do?"

There was such a note of defeat in the old lawyer's voice. He sounded like a man who wasn't sure of himself. A man who maybe had trouble sleeping at night. But there was also desperation and compassion. Logan had absolutely no doubt that Bella's father was doing this for all the right reasons. Just as Logan had no doubt that it weighed heavily on the man's conscience.

For the first time in his life, Logan actually felt compassion for the man who he'd once regarded as his nemesis.

He actually felt sorry for him.

"She's happy now, Logan." The old man twisted the

knife a little harder.

“I don’t know… that’s all the commitment I can give to you now. Don’t worry, I’m not going to blurt it out next time I see her but I have to take this as it comes.”

Logan swore he could hear the sigh of relief echoing all the way down the line from Melbourne. A paltry three thousand kilometres away.

“Okay.”

“But if she remembers… if she asks me… I *won’t* lie to her, Graham.”

The older man’s swallow was audible. “Fair enough,” he said, his voice unsteady.

“Would you have told her? If she’d asked?” Logan needed to know suddenly. Needed to know more than his next breath.

“I… don’t know.”

It was the most genuine thing Logan had ever heard come out of Tucker Senior’s mouth. He could easily have lied. But the man who had once been an overprotective father with wealth and power and connections was now just a man who’d lived through something no father ever wanted to live through.

“Well, I guess that puts us both on the same page for once,” Logan said.

“How does that feel?” he asked, the humour in his voice barely perceptible.

Logan snorted. “Not as good as I thought it would.”

"Same here."

There was another moment of pregnant silence then the phone hung up in his ear.

Chapter Three

ARABELLA WAS FIFTEEN minutes later than even she'd predicted. She could see the sign for Rosie's up ahead but her old hip injury didn't allow for a lot of dashing around. She could already feel it protesting at her increased pace.

She had no idea why she was hurrying. The guy she'd met on the street today – Logan – would surely have already left by now. She doubted a guy as good-looking as he was used to women standing him up.

Hell, she wasn't sure why she'd even suggested they meet. Because he was sexy seemed a really bad reason to meet up with a guy she didn't know. Even though she apparently did…

Mostly though, she was curious. She'd *known* this guy? Now *that* was a memory she could have done with!

She'd contemplated ringing her mother and asking if she knew who he might be but had decided against it. Her parents had already been antsy about her temporary relocation to Brisbane and she didn't want to worry them anymore. And, besides, if he was someone she knew from when she'd lived here once upon a time, her parents probably didn't know him anyway.

Not that it would matter if he'd tired of waiting for her and left.

Her stomach tightened in nervous anticipation. She hoped not. Ignoring the ache in her hip, she sped up the last half block and pushed the heavy wooden door of the bar open a minute later.

The cool kiss of air-conditioning was a blissful reprieve from the oppressive warmth of late afternoon/early evening. The yeasty aroma of beer greeted her as she glanced around, squinting as her eyes adjusted from the still bright day outside to the dimmer light inside the wood-panelled surroundings.

"Bella!"

She glanced in the direction of his voice to see him half standing at an end booth. He waved at her and smiled, his whole face lighting up, and it almost stole her breath.

Lordy. This man should be locked up. A smile that could surely cause mass ovulation *had* to be illegal.

She concentrated on keeping her gait as even as possible as she walked towards him rather than his intense gaze. He didn't take his eyes off her and her heart fibrillated like a Richter scale needle during an earthquake as she grew closer.

The moment felt kind of seismic too. Like the earth shifting under her feet.

"Bella," he said again as she drew level with the booth.

Bloody hell! The way he said her name, with a soft "a" at the end, stretching it out as if he was savouring it. Halfway between a sigh and a caress that travelled all the way down to her toes and back up again. Sucking in a shaky breath, she slid into the booth opposite him.

"Can I get you a drink?"

"Thanks." She nodded. "A glass of pinot grigio would be lovely."

He headed to the bar and she tracked his progress as he ate up the distance. His legs, as long as a summer's day, were encased in dark navy trousers that looked hard wearing and kind of military with all the pockets and zips. There were reflective strips running down the side seam and the fabric stretched nice and taut across his ass. His navy, short-sleeved shirt rose from the narrow line of his hips to fit snug around his shoulders.

Shoulders that'd give a woman something to hold on to.

His chest filled the shirt just as nicely as he made his way back to the table. Her gaze ran up the row of buttons to the open collar exposing the dark dusting of five o'clock shadow on his tanned neck and strong jawline. There were smooth hollows beneath his cheekbones and his dark brown hair had been cropped into submission close to his scalp.

But it was the sexy cleft in his chin that drew her gaze. Her fingertips itched to trace it; her tongue salivated to taste it.

He slid the glass of wine onto the table in front of her and Arabella noticed the tanned, corded muscles of his forearms. She was hyperaware, too, of the press of his thighs against the taut fabric of his trousers and how temptingly close they were.

For a moment, the sheer masculinity of his presence swamped her, her nostrils flaring with a scent that was even more base than beer. The urgent desire to pull his head down and kiss him flickered like a lit match out of the blue. Thankfully, he was sliding into his side of the booth before she could action the crazy impulse.

But her hand shook from the near miss, her pulse fluttering from the startling fierceness of the whim.

Her cheeks warmed as she reached for a fortifying sip of the wine, her gaze not quite able to reach his, settling instead on a point mid-chest. An embroidered row of red stitching on his left pec came into focus. It announced he worked for Urban Fire Services.

A lot of the men in the pub were wearing similar shirts – obviously Rosie's was popular with the fire service.

Above it, in larger capitals was, she assumed, his surname.

Knight.

Unless they'd bestowed that title on all firefighters these days. Which, considering the kind of bravery they must exhibit day in and day out, wasn't such a bad idea.

But Logan Knight didn't look like a shiny armour kind

of guy. She had no doubt he'd rescued many the damsel from a burning tower using those big, broad shoulders but there was something downright dirty about that fascinating cleft in his chin.

Too dirty for shiny that was for damn sure.

"Knight," she said, realising she was staring at his chest. "That's your surname?"

"Yes." He placed his beer on the table.

Arabella frowned as something niggled at the back of her brain. "Knight…" Where had she heard that name recently? Oh, yes, on the news. "Are you any relation to Commissioner Knight who died a few weeks ago?"

His eyebrows raised in faint surprise. "Yes. He was my grandfather."

"Oh…" she murmured. "I'm so sorry."

Her grandfather might be an old curmudgeon but she loved him dearly and would be very sad when he died. She quashed an urge to reach across and touch his arm. It might have been a natural sympathetic gesture but every female instinct Arabella owned warned her that touching him would be dangerous.

That she might not want to stop.

Still, it was awkward *not* doing it.

"Thank you." He smiled, if a little bleakly. "He'll be missed."

The sincerity in Logan's words was palpable. "So… fire fighting is in the Knight genes?"

He gave a self-deprecating half-snort, half-laugh. "You could say that. My grandfather, my father, my many uncles and just about every cousin I own. And me, who's been very rude and not introduced myself properly."

"You do have me at a disadvantage."

Arabella swore she meant it in the most innocent way. But the quirk of his lips chased away the last remnants of sadness from his face, deepening the cleft. There was nothing innocent about how he'd taken it.

Like having her at a disadvantage could be a whole lot of fun.

Still, he held out his hand all nice and polite. "A pleasure to meet you, ma'am. My name's Logan James Knight."

Arabella glanced at his hand. Her head screamed a warning – just looking at the man was tempting enough and the way he'd said *pleasure*…

But she didn't seem to be able to stop herself either.

Not touching him before had felt awkward and ignoring his hand now would just be plain rude.

Riding a sudden streak of recklessness, she slipped her hand into his. On cue, the grimy sounds of Kings of Leon singing about sex on fire insinuated themselves into her head.

She cleared her throat of its sudden constriction. "Arabella Tucker."

He regarded her for a moment or two, her palm burning from his touch, before he gave a half laugh and slid his hand away. "You were always Bella to me."

The rich vein of possession in his voice was enthralling but it was the undercurrent of wistfulness that broke her heart.

"We weren't just… friends, were we?"

He took a slug of his beer, his gaze assessing over the rim of the glass. For a moment she thought he was going to lie, or maybe obfuscate and it was unbearable.

"Please don't," she said, leaning forward, extending her hand across the table in some kind of a beseeching gesture. "Don't lie to me."

Her parents had meant well, always trying to contain and control the information coming at her so it wasn't overwhelming but she was stronger than they gave her credit for and she didn't want this man to treat her like she might break.

She shot him a small smile. "I can handle the truth."

He placed his half full glass on the table, his mind clearly made up. She withdrew her hand. "No. We weren't just friends."

Arabella's pulse spiked. "So we…" She waved her hand vaguely in the air. The thought of what they might have done together coloured her cheeks and stole all her air.

She had no breath left to give voice to the images in her head.

One side of his mouth quirked, the wicked cleft confirming she was on the right page. "Yes."

Her breath escaped on a rush. *They'd been lovers.* This man had been her lover and she *didn't remember.*

Amnesia had been a frustrating condition to live with but Arabella had resigned herself some time ago to the hole it had left in her life. And she'd honestly thought she was through the worst of it.

She'd been wrong.

Christ. How could she *not* remember him? How could she feel completely sucker-punched, how could her body be more alive than it had been since she'd woken from her coma four years ago, and yet not remember they'd been here before?

Logan Knight – to all intents and purposes a complete stranger – had been her lover.

"You… don't remember, then?"

Arabella shook her head. He'd gone still suddenly. His jaw tight, his gaze wary.

"I'm sorry." God, how many times had she said those words these last four years? "I wish that I did but…"

She shook her head again. It was too hard to explain. Too hard to comprehend. *She* didn't understand it most of the time and she was living it.

"It's okay." His smile was gentle but there was a bleakness to it as well. "It's not your fault."

That was true. And God knew she'd heard it a thousand times. But it *felt* like her fault. Like maybe, she wasn't trying hard enough. Like maybe, if she concentrated just a little bit more she might remember.

Arabella would never have thought that the simple act of remembering – or trying to in her case – could be so damn exhausting.

She was so *over* trying to remember.

"Well…" She didn't know what else to say. What could she say to a man who wore their memories on his sleeve? She glanced at his chest. "At least I had good taste back then."

He blinked and seemed taken aback for a beat or two then threw back his head and laughed.

Man. His laugh. Deep and throaty. A rich, husky baritone. It washed over her like a caress.

She clapped a hand over her mouth. "Sorry. I didn't mean to say that out loud."

She'd just meant to bridge the silence but she should know from bitter experience, amnesia-related silence could never really be bridged.

"I think we both had good taste," he said graciously once his merriment had settled. And like that, the mood shifted, the gloom lifted.

"So… you're a fireman?"

He looked down at his uniform. "Yes ma'am."

Arabella smiled. Working in the legal system she was well used to being called ma'am but he somehow gave the respectability of it a dirty edge.

"Have you always been in the service?"

"Nine years. Since I was twenty."

So he was a year older than her. Had he been a firefighter when she knew him the first time around or had that come after? "And have you always been stationed in Brisbane?"

"No. I've actually just come back from a few years of rural work out west and I spent two years in the US working in Montana."

"But you were stationed here when we met? I presume we met in Brisbane?"

He hesitated. "Yes."

Arabella was used to people hesitating when discussing her past and it drove her nutty.

Somehow, she'd thought he'd be different. "You don't sound too sure?"

He let out a breath. "I'm not sure what I can tell you. If I'm allowed to tell you… stuff."

Arabella laughed. "Relax. It's not like the movies. I'm not going to have some kind of seizure if you fill in the gaps for me."

He smiled at her attempt at humour and seemed to relax again. "I started my rookie year here when I came back from a Contiki tour, which is where I met you."

Arabella's eyes widened. "*You* were on my Contiki tour?"

She frowned, mentally cataloguing the photos she'd seen from that trip. She didn't recall him being in any of them. She might have amnesia but she remembered *everything* she'd been told and shown since her accident and she was damn sure she'd remember him!

"Yep."

"I don't remember you being in any of my photos."

He shrugged. "You're in all of mine."

"Really? I'd like to see them some time."

"Of course. If you want."

If she wanted? Arabella wanted far too much where this man was concerned.

He took another mouthful of his beer, his tanned forearms flexing in her direct line of sight and Arabella's belly heated. "So… we had a good time… together?"

His slow smile warmed his eyes and lit a fire in her veins, the sexy cleft confirming what she'd already guessed from the insane amount of chemistry smouldering like a tyre factory fire between them.

How could she feel it so powerfully and yet not remember it?

"We had a *very* good time together."

Her belly clenched violently. *God.* They'd fucked like bunnies, hadn't they? She had a sudden admiration for nineteen-year-old Arabella.

You go, girl.

"Were you the reason I lived in Brisbane after I came back from Europe?"

"Yes."

Arabella's pulse picked up. Her parents had told her that she'd decided to take a belated gap year. It hadn't seemed like something she would have done but she understood why now.

Logan was a gap year wet dream.

"We lived together?"

"Yes."

Her breath hitched. She wished she'd quizzed her parents more closely on that now. But when she hadn't been able to remember she'd even *taken* a gap year, she hadn't seen the point in asking for the details. Why dwell on a place and time as far removed from her post-amnesia reality as the vast distance that separated Brisbane and Melbourne?

She ran her gaze over his arms, up his chest, and across his shoulders. He was broad and strong. Muscled. Tanned. His hands were big and capable looking. The type that knew their way around a car engine or a toolbox as well as a woman's body. Rough and perfect on breasts and stomach and thighs. So far removed from the soft, manicured hands of the men who populated her world.

Lordy. Even his hands got her hot under the collar.

Logan Knight was as blue-collar as football, meat pies, kangaroos, and Holden cars. No wonder her parents hadn't elaborated. She doubted they'd approved. "My parents couldn't have been too impressed."

He smiled but it was tight. It didn't warm his eyes or show off his chin dimple. "You could say that."

He was being polite. Treading very carefully.

Arabella didn't feel similarly restrained. "What happened to us?"

He contemplated her for long moments, raw emotion on full display in the cloudy grey of his eyes. *He would suck at being a lawyer.*

"We were… young," he said eventually, his gaze locking with hers.

For a moment she thought he was going to leave it at that. As if their youth was an explanation in itself.

He didn't.

"And stupid. And impulsive. And immature. We had passion but were too young to understand a relationship needed more than that. I think we were doomed to unravel right from the beginning. And when it came to the crunch… we didn't fight for us."

His words burrowed under her skin. Arabella couldn't look away from the rawness and honesty in his gaze, the hubbub of the pub fading to nothing. His insight was startling. She'd known divorcing couples who'd been married for decades who couldn't articulate what had gone wrong.

"That sounds sad," Arabella murmured.

He nodded. "It was."

The words were simple but weighty; the well of emotion dammed up behind them a physical force against her chest.

He'd loved her. The thought almost stopped her heart. This man was a stranger to her yet she'd never been surer of anything. "I'm sorry."

He gave a half shrug as a ghost of a smile flitted across his mouth. "It wasn't meant to be."

Maybe… but what about now? She'd known him for less than five hours yet the tug she felt when she looked at him was real. The flutter of her pulse and the twist in her gut was *very* real. She could barely breathe from the thick, hot air singeing her lungs. It was a dozen kinds of crazy.

If she didn't lighten this up, she was going to burst into flames where she sat.

Just as well she was surrounded by firefighters.

"That's not going to stop me from going through my Contiki pictures again with a fine-tooth comb."

He smiled and the tension eased. "I suspect you have no photos of me for a reason."

Arabella quirked an eyebrow she'd only recently had threaded. "You think I deleted them all in some kind of fit of spurned lover pique?"

Had she? Had she been that cut up by their relationship ending that she'd deleted every trace of him from her life? It made sense as to why there were no pictures. But it didn't sound like the kind of thing she would do either.

He laughed. "Maybe."

"Ha." She smiled. "If only I'd known I was going to get amnesia a few years later. I could have saved myself the trouble."

He laughed out loud, reaching for his beer and took a mouthful. The tanned column of his throat bobbed and Arabella wished like hell she remembered how it felt to run her tongue up the strong ridge of his trachea. What he smelled like there.

"Tell me about the accident," he said, placing his beer on the table, obviously changing the subject.

Arabella didn't want to talk about the accident. She wanted to know more about them. *Everything* about them. The stuff that had went right as well as the stuff that had gone wrong. She sure as hell wanted to know more about their *passion*. But she could let it drop for now. She didn't need a crystal ball to tell her she was going to be seeing a hell of a lot more of this man.

Both in the dating sense and the naked sense.

She'd find out the story of them in time.

Chapter Four

"I WAS HIT by a speeding car on my bicycle riding to uni. Bounced off the windscreen, tossed in the air, landed on the opposite side of the road."

His fingers tightened around the glass and he winced. "Christ. That must have been…"

"It's okay." Arabella smiled. "Best part about amnesia? I don't remember any of it."

"Injuries?"

"Fractured pelvis, fractured ribs, fractured left ankle, fractured left femur, fractured left humerus and clavicle, a collapsed left lung, a head injury." She took a breath. "And a partridge in a pear tree."

He didn't seem to find it funny, his grey eyes serious – intense.

"Fuck," he whispered, paling beneath his tan.

"Indeed." Arabella grinned because she was alive and all better now.

"What kind of a head injury?"

"Closed. Small subdural haematoma they managed conservatively."

"Bad enough to knock out nine years of your life, though."

"Yes. But it could have been a lot worse had I not been wearing a helmet." The doctors had told her she'd have probably died without one.

"You seem to have recovered from it okay apart from the memory?"

"I was in a bit of a neurological fog for a couple of months after. Very confused. And my speech and cognitive function was mildly affected. But I slowly recovered from that."

"Is it possible that you might recover from the amnesia too?"

His voice was light but she could see the whitening at the angle of his jaw and the tension in his shoulders. He clearly *wanted* her to remember. Hell, sitting opposite God's gift to women, she wanted it too. She wanted to remember every second with this man. She wanted it all back. *Everything.* Even the bad stuff.

But… she'd given up wishing for something that was never going to be. It'd been hard but she'd abandoned hope. And whatever happened from here on out with her and Logan it was important that she didn't give him any reason to hope either.

"No." She locked her gaze with his. "It's not."

"But the brain's a complex thing, right? So who really

knows? And there must be new treatments coming out all the time?"

Arabella shook her head. "There is no treatment for amnesia."

He dropped his gaze to his beer for a moment before returning his attention to her face shooting her an apologetic smile. "Right. Sorry. So… what about your limp? Is that pelvis, the leg, or the ankle?"

Arabella smiled back, thankful to him for dropping it when she could see how hard it was for him to grasp. "The pelvis. Mainly."

"I imagine that took a little longer to recover from."

She sipped her wine. "Two years of physio. But then my physiotherapist was kinda hot so I'm not entirely sure I wasn't malingering for the last six months or so."

He quirked an eyebrow at her. "You're chipper for someone who was pretty banged up for two years and can't remember a huge chunk of her life."

Arabella laughed and quickly covered her mouth as his brows knotted together. "You sound like my eighty-year-old grandfather." Except Logan was fit and vital and even all stern looking he oozed sex appeal. Whereas her grandfather's face bore more of a resemblance to an old boot.

He blinked. "Christ. I did, didn't I?" He ran a hand through his hair. "Sorry, I don't usually have a stick jammed up my butt."

"I'm alive, Logan," she said, reaching across the table and

squeezing his forearm.

The muscle tensed beneath her palm, hinting at the power leashed there. Involuntarily, her fingernails curled into the warm skin. His gaze zeroed in on her hand before shifting to her face. Her lips lost all their moisture as her tongue flicked over her mouth.

"Yes," he murmured. "You are."

Her hand was still on his arm but he made no attempt to shake her off. They were having a moment. Intense. Personal. Private.

In the middle of a busy inner-city bar.

All their history sat large between them and even though she was a stranger to it, she could sense its presence.

How was it possible to feel so attracted to this man she'd obviously once known *very* well but not be familiar with him at the same time? Not still have some sense of that?

Fanciful ideas of fated lovers tripped through her mind. Maybe their destinies had always been entwined. How else did she explain the fact that not even nine years and a case of amnesia had kept them apart?

But she was only here temporarily. For about three months depending on her work. And two weeks of that had already slipped away. She had a home and a job and a life in Melbourne. She was happy there.

Was it fair to succumb to whatever the hell this was when it was clear Logan had already been devastated once by what had gone down between them?

She withdrew her hand, a sense of loss and regret swamping her. There was a beat or two of awkward silence as they both sipped their drinks.

"You went on to finish your law degree," he said after long moments. "I'm impressed."

"Oh no." She dismissed the suggestion with a toss of her head. "I'm not a lawyer."

"Oh. You said you had to get back to court so I just assumed…"

Arabella shook her head. It had been her goal at fifteen and she had, apparently, been finishing up her law degree when she'd been hit by the car. But she hadn't remembered any of her uni years and she was damned after two years of intense therapy if she was going to go and relearn all she'd forgotten, no matter how much her father had pushed for it.

Relearning basic functions had been hard enough.

"I'm a paralegal. I work for my dad's firm."

He nodded casually but she was already noticing even tiny details about him. Like the tightening at the angle of his jaw.

"It was easy to pick up and a lot less stressful when I was finally able enough to contribute to society again. Besides, what good are family connections if you can't pump them, right?"

She smiled at him and her insides dissolved into a puddle when he smiled back.

"So what brings you to Brisbane?"

"The firm's involved in a big civil class action suit up here that's scheduled to run for few months. The barrister that's handling the case needed a team to accompany him and I volunteered."

"Because?"

Arabella shrugged. "I don't know." It was the honest truth.

She hadn't thought about it overly at the time. The opportunity had arisen and it had appealed to her but with some distance she could see she'd been craving a change.

"I guess I felt like I was… treading water and I wanted to stretch my wings a bit. I'd been in Collins Street for two years and I was feeling restless, I suppose. We were having a heinous summer and a few months in sunny Brisbane sounded like bliss."

Maybe it was destiny. Maybe she'd been fated to come to Brisbane so she could cross paths with Logan again. She didn't really believe in any of that stuff but she couldn't deny their reunion had been freakishly coincidental.

Nor could she deny the strong sexual attraction buzzing between them. She'd felt it on the street earlier, the second his hand had touched her arm but it had seemed… fanciful. Sitting opposite him right now it was *very freaking real.* The urge to lean across the table, grab the front of his shirt, and lay a kiss on his mouth, couldn't be so easily dismissed.

She wanted nothing more than to invite him back to her place and get to know him again in *all* the ways possible.

She curled her fingers into the red leather of the booth seat.

"And there you were," he said, his gaze intense as it searched hers, "outside my firehouse, as if you knew I was inside."

The hairs on the back of Arabella's neck prickled as the muscles on either side cranked tight. Hope and expectation glimmered in his eyes. Her chest constricted as dread ran hot and cold through her veins. She'd seen this before, too often. In the eyes of her family and friends, hoping something they did or said might trigger a memory for her or unlock the vault where the mother lode of those missing years was being kept hostage.

Their crushing disappointment when it didn't happen had been hard to bear. And the guilt that she couldn't remember – for them, the people she loved most in the world – had been exhausting.

"No, Logan." She shook her head. She had to quash any idea he might have that she'd somehow been drawn to the building by a suppressed memory. "I just really love old architecture. Must be the Melbourne girl in me." She shot him a self-deprecating smile. "The building is beautiful. And those big red doors are so eye-catching."

"So you didn't –"

"No." She cut him off. "I didn't recognise it. It doesn't *mean* anything to me."

"Okay, sure," he said, slowly nodding his head disguising

his disappointment well but disappointment was something Arabella was particularly attuned to. "It is kinda random though, don't you think?"

"Life's random," she dismissed, neck muscles clenched tight, because the fact that the universe had brought them together for a second time seemed eerily *calculated* rather than random.

"Yeah. I guess," he mused. "Still, it's very strange meeting up again like this. It feels… weird."

Welcome to my life, buddy.

She smiled but it felt strained. "Yes… well… amnesia *is* weird."

"I know, right? Like… why fifteen? Why cut off there? Do the doctors know?"

"Nope. They have no idea why."

"How did they even pinpoint that? Is there some kind of scan for that?"

Arabella laughed. "Nothing as sophisticated as that. It's a simple case of elimination, really. I remember my fifteenth birthday because some friends and I went to St. Kilda Beach for the day. But a week later the family went to Bali for a holiday and I don't remember any of it or anything past it until I woke up in hospital. I don't remember finishing high school or going to university or the Contiki tour or my sister getting married or my two nieces being born."

He hunched forward, regarding her and she braced herself for more questions she couldn't answer and more disappointment she couldn't control.

But, after a long moment he relaxed back and half smiled. "Weird."

"You have *no* idea."

His gaze roved over her face, probing and insightful. The struggle she'd seen in his eyes as he'd grappled with his disappointment suddenly smoothed out. "Oh, yeah?"

He smiled, his cleft dimpling deliciously at her and the muscles either side of Arabella's neck melted like marshmallow.

"Yeah. There's been a *lot* of weird conversations with people that I was supposed to know but didn't. Or about things I couldn't remember doing."

He laughed all low and easy and it soothed the residual ache in her neck muscles. "What's the weirdest?"

Heat flooded her cheeks as the weirdest came readily to mind. Arabella appreciated the effort he was making to put his own feelings aside and pull her out of her funk but that conversation was probably best left in the past, never to be repeated. "Oh no, it's too embarrassing."

"The mind boggles," he mused, a small smile playing across his mouth.

The laughter in his tone warmed her right down to the pit of her stomach.

"You know they say confession is good for the soul right?"

"I don't think that applies unless you're a priest. And you

don't look like *any* priest I've ever seen."

"It's true, I am having trouble with purity of thoughts at the moment," he admitted, laughter infusing his voice with just the right note of flirtation.

Not too heavy, not too needy. But there if she wanted to pick it up and play.

And God help her, Arabella wanted to play.

She hadn't had a pure thought since she'd met him. Again.

"But you should know, I'm a very good listener and I promise not to laugh."

Their gazes locked. But for the table, Arabella would actually have leaned in a little more. She sucked in a breath which wasn't big enough to fill the burgeoning capacity of her lungs.

Dear God. She wanted to tell him. "Well… it was more awkward than weird."

"Awkward. Check," he said, his voice serious, his chin smooth, no hint of dimple.

"I had to…" Her cheeks warmed again remembering it. "Ask my sister if I was a virgin."

He didn't bat an eyelid. His lips didn't twitch. His eyebrows didn't move. "And?"

"She confirmed I wasn't but had no idea who I'd lost it to."

Their gazes locked for long moments. He was straight-faced, his features calm and collected, carefully schooled at the revelation, like she'd just told him the sky was blue or something equally inane.

It was too much. Arabella broke first, her lips twitching at the absurdity of sharing something so private and personal with a guy who, for all intents and purposes, had been a stranger six hours ago.

She cracked first and he joined her. "You promised you wouldn't do that," she accused.

"You started it." He chuckled.

"Oh, God," Arabella said, half snorting as her laughter came to an abrupt halt at the realisation of a horrible possibility. "I didn't lose it to you, did I?"

"No. You lost it to a guy called Travis Conner at uni in O week. You were eighteen."

"Oh, my God!" Arabella blushed. "I *told* you that?"

A tiny flinch flickered across his features but his smile stayed firmly in place. "We didn't have any secrets."

Arabella didn't doubt it. She'd known him for approximately six hours and she wanted to tell this man *everything*. "Well? Was he any good? Did I enjoy it?"

"You said he was a perfectly adequate lover," Logan supplied, a small smile masking the bigger one he was clearly trying to hold back.

"Perfectly adequate?" Arabella's heart banged hard against her ribcage as she stared at his mouth, a hint of his prowess in their fullness. "I don't suppose I ever said that about you?"

She only had to look at Logan and those rough hands of his to know he'd be a thoroughly, mind-blowingly, head-bangingly, dirty lover.

"I bloody hope not."

Arabella's toes curled in her shoes. *Actually curled.* She blushed again and changed the subject. "And did you tell me who you lost yours to?"

"I did."

"And?"

"I'm not sure I should kiss and tell. Twice."

"Oh, come on, you know mine. I think it's only fair I know yours."

He shook his head in mock seriousness, his grey eyes dancing. "You barely know me."

Arabella sucked in a breath at his teasing. Something expanded in her chest. Something big and warm, wrapping tentacles around her heart.

She bet she'd laughed a lot with this guy. She quirked an eyebrow. "So let's start with this."

"Fine." He sighed, his smile amplifying his charisma tenfold. "Her name was Molly. She was the daughter of one of my father's fire buddies. I was sixteen, she was seventeen."

"Oooh." Her eyes teased him as she drained the last of her wine. "An older woman."

He grinned. "Well one of us had to know what we were doing."

Arabella laughed. "Right, like you weren't born knowing."

He grinned but didn't refute her statement. She found it hard to believe a guy who oozed sex didn't just *know* shit like that. The man was practically melting her underwear off from his proximity alone. Add in the smile, the chin cleft, and his delicious banter and she was virtually commando.

Still, there was something endearing about a guy who freely admitted to a lack of sexual expertise without it mortally wounding his personality.

"So…" He shot her a speculative glance over the top of his beer, draining it before placing it back on the table. "I guess that means that you got to be a virgin all over again?"

"Well, not technically, there was Travis after all. And… you."

Arabella held her breath as his gaze drifted to her mouth then back up again, a flash of heat like summer lightning sizzling in his grey eyes. "I'm really not sure you should count Travis." She noted he didn't discount himself. "I hope the second guy was better than perfectly adequate," he teased.

Arabella had dated occasionally in the last couple of years including a fling with a visiting associate from the firm's Sydney office. He'd been the first guy she'd slept with after the accident. There'd been two more since.

"Well, I didn't really have anything to compare him to but it was nice."

He blinked. "*Nice*?"

Arabella smiled at his curled lip. He looked like nice was an offence to the whole sexual act. It was almost comical. "Yes. *Nice.* Not every guy can be a Casanova in the bedroom, you know."

Frankly, she'd just been glad she could manage it without aggravating her hip. There was nothing like the thought of pain or injury to put a dampener on both spontaneity and the urge to be adventurous.

Not that she felt any such restrictions under Logan's continuing gaze. Something told her a dislocated hip would be a small price to pay for twisting herself into a pretzel with him.

"Maybe," he murmured, "but I think you can do better than *nice.*"

Arabella sucked in a breath thick as syrup. He didn't need to say that he'd happily volunteer; she could see it in the flare of heat in his eyes. She knew it in her gut.

"I'd like that," she said.

He hadn't specifically offered, she hadn't specifically accepted but it was out there now. Sex hung between them, shiny and tantalising, waiting for one of them to reach out and take it. Arabella knew where this was heading. It was just a matter of time.

He cleared his throat. "You want another?" He pointed at her empty glass.

Arabella shook her head. If she had another wine, sex would be more than just an eventuality between them. He'd be lucky to get out of here without a bathroom quickie. "I really should get going. I have a lot of work to get through for tomorrow still."

It wasn't an excuse. She *did* have a lot of research to do from scribbled notes she'd taken today.

If Logan was disappointed he didn't show it. He just said, "Where are you staying?"

"At some apartments in Mary Street."

"Okay." He stood. "I'll walk you back."

Arabella also stood. She didn't protest his propriety. An hour in his company and she knew it was the kind of guy Logan Knight was.

And damned if that wasn't a turn on too.

Chapter Five

AN INKY TWILIGHT had fallen across the city. Streets glowed with the neon of signs and traffic lights. Stars winked overhead and the silvery promise of moonlight bathed the tops of the skyscrapers. A light breeze ruffled Arabella's hair, bathing her in sultry Brisbane heat.

Logan talked as they walked, mainly about the buildings they passed adding in some fire-related anecdotes to flourish it. It was an interesting way to see the city as she kept pace to the resonance of his deep, rich voice.

Where she saw the beauty of architecture, he saw the potential dangers. She supposed as someone charged with having to put fires out of said buildings, it was an occupational hazard to analyse their weak points and always have an action plan at the ready. It wasn't a very romantic view but fighting fires was hardly the stuff romance was made of.

It looked hot and hard and dangerous. Real life-on-the-line stuff.

Even the thought of the dangers moved her closer to him.

Their arms brushed and she made no attempt to put space between them. He made no attempt either. Her heart pounded at the contact, her whole body coming alive, buzzing with the promise of something beautiful. And when his hand slipped into hers it seemed like the most natural thing in the world to curl her fingers around his.

"So, you really don't remember any of this?" he asked, flinging his spare arm out to encompass the cityscape.

Arabella looked around her at the city so obviously embedded into his DNA. She wished she did but the truth was nothing about the streets and buildings were familiar.

"I really don't." She kept her response light, as the question had been, despite the knot forming between her shoulder blades. She had to remember that she'd thrown Logan for a loop and he needed time to wrap his head around it. She was four years ahead of him in this process.

She was at acceptance. He was still at denial.

"Not even the alleyways? We made out in a *lot* of alleyways."

She laughed and the knot dissolved, her pulse tripping at the thought of them not being able to keep their hands off each other. *Lordy*. How was it possible to be turned on by something she couldn't recall? She glanced up to find him grinning. She shook her head at him and he laughed, low and sexy, and damn if that didn't turn her on too.

A few minutes later, they reached her apartment building, stopping in the middle of the footpath and just staring at each other. Arabella's heart beat double-time and her breath hitched as a low, slow pulse throbbed to life between her legs.

"I can't believe it's you," Logan said, shaking his head.

A group of guys, laughing and joking and reeking of booze, pushed around them and Logan grabbed her hand and pulled her into the shadows between the outside wall and a row of trees that had been planted to grow up through the footpath.

Arabella settled herself against the wall, her shoulder blades nudging the warm stone of the building. He stepped in closer, his hands landing on her waist, his thighs aligning with hers. She sucked in a breath at the delicious heat transferring from his to hers.

His aroma swirled around her. God, he smelled *primal.*

Very, *very* male. With a faint trace of something sweet that might have come from a bottle. Something elusive that made her want to bury her face in his neck to investigate thoroughly.

"Is this how it was?" she asked, her voice tremulous, searching his gaze for the same kind of crazy that had her in its grip. Her pulse tripped madly at her temple and washed through her ears. "Back then. Between us? This… madness? This… compulsion?"

He nodded, his hands tightening on her hips. "Right from the start. You got on that bus in London and I…" He smiled and she could see the memory glowing in his gaze despite the poor light. "I was a goner."

She shook her head, trying to clear it of the clash of sensations agitating around inside – lust and sex and desire warring with common sense and propriety and a weird feeling of dislocation.

She didn't know this man. Nothing was familiar about him. *Nothing.* The attraction was intense – also completely insane – but it was *new*. She had no doubts about it.

"It's crazy how much I want to kiss you right now," she whispered, her hands sliding around his neck of their own volition.

"Then kiss me."

Arabella didn't need any more urging, pushing up on her tippy toes, his warm breath fanning across her cheek as her mouth met his. It was hard against hers and the kiss was hot and deep and sure right from the start. The kiss of a man who'd done this with the same woman a thousand times before.

Who knew *how* she liked to be kissed.

And Arabella liked it very much.

She moaned as his tongue demanded entry. The hot tang of his skin, the bulk of his chest and thighs, the husk of his breath all overwhelmed her senses. She moved restlessly, instinctively, parting her legs to welcome the thick, strong solidity of a thigh pressing hard and urgent just where she needed it. She rubbed against him and his groan echoed through her bones, flooding her body with a tidal wave of lust.

He tasted like beer and he was solid and hot against her and she wanted him to ruck her skirt up and do her against this wall. The heat where his thigh was wedged roared like a wildfire.

"Christ, Bella," he muttered, breaking off to press his forehead to hers. "I've missed you."

Arabella didn't know what to say as she chugged in much needed oxygen. She hadn't missed him, but she knew for damn sure she missed the press of his mouth – the urgent havoc of it – already. So she sought his lips again, kissing him wet and deep, her hands clamped firm on the back of his head, holding him captive, grinding against the pressure of his quad lodged at the juncture of her thighs.

She wasn't sure if it was minutes or only moments later that someone called, "Get a room," followed by a loud wolf whistle. He wrenched his mouth away, angling his torso back slightly, his hands anchoring firmly on her hip bones.

His breathing was choppy with desire and despite the darkened corner she could feel the probe of his gaze searching hers. "Ask me up."

The request was so ragged it felt tangible, as if he'd dragged his fingers across her nipples. It infused her senses with lust, muddling her head until she couldn't think straight.

Going to bed with a guy she'd only just met – for all intents and purposes – wasn't something she did.

Ever.

She didn't care if others chose to, having sex with guys she barely knew just wasn't for her. Or she hadn't thought so anyway. In fact, until today, she'd have said her sexual experience was fairly limited.

Although apparently she'd been to bed with Logan, *plenty*.

Every cell in her body wanted her to say yes. To throw caution and everything she thought she knew about herself out the window and do something totally wild. Hell, she felt *reckless* just looking at him. But…

She took a shaky breath. "I… can't." Who'd have thought two simple words could be so damn hard to force out of her mouth?

"God. Sorry… forget I asked." He shook his head, his voice husky. "That was… I'm a caveman. Apologies, I just…"

Yeah. She understood exactly what he *just*. She'd been in the moment too, drowning alongside him. "No. *I'm* sorry. It's just that… I don't know you and–"

He stiffened. Given how jammed tight their bodies still were it was easy to detect.

"I'm sorry," she said, sliding a hand to cup his jaw. "I didn't mean…" She felt helpless.

This had to be hard for him – in more ways than the one she could feel pressing thick and insistent against her belly.

"I need some time to wrap my head around this. And

besides… I *really* do have a lot of work I need to get through so we're ready for court tomorrow."

If she asked Logan into her apartment they'd end up in her bed and there'd be no work done tonight.

Not of the legal kind anyway.

"Of course." He took a step back, his hands leaving her hips, one of them raking through his hair. "I got a little carried away."

A little? If that was a little then Arabella couldn't wait to be the focus when he got *a lot* carried away. Her toes curled at the thought.

"But–" She took a step closer to him, already missing the heat and hardness of him. "I can… I need to eat lunch tomorrow. I can always do that in my usual spot."

He smiled at her, sexy and sad all at once. "I go on five night shifts starting tomorrow night."

"Oh."

Instantly images of Logan lying asleep and naked on his bed, his body bathed in daylight all day for five long days, crowded out everything else. The low simmer of desire bubbling like a cauldron in her pelvis kicked up a notch.

Man. This was crazy. Clearly, she needed a break from him to sort her head out. Five days should be long enough.

Probably…

"I finish Sunday morning. Maybe you could…"

Come over and rock you to sleep? Arabella placed a hand just below her sternum to still the riot as she straddled him in her mind, his hips squeezed between her thighs.

"Meet me for breakfast? There's a great place down on the river that does a mean eggs Benedict."

Her heart, still not settled from their wild pash session, leapt. Eggs Benedict. Her favourite. Always had been. How did he…?

But of course. Something else this stranger-she-wanted-inside-her-so-badly-her-legs-trembled knew about her. What was his breakfast food of choice? She squinted slightly as she forced herself to concentrate, to look inward, to peer back into the dark void of her amnesia.

Nope. Nothing.

Her sense of discombobulation intensified.

"Or do they make you work on the weekend too?" he asked as the silence stretched between them, a small smile playing on his lips, the cleft in his chin winking at her.

"No. Breakfast is good."

Breakfast was more than good. It was the sensible option. Much more so than riding him like a cowgirl.

She'd asked him for time to wrap her head around it and he was giving it to her. Breakfast was a perfectly above board, in full-view-of-the-public, platonic option. Frankly, she didn't care. She just wanted to see him again.

"But… won't you be too tired?"

He shook his head, his hands crammed into his pockets, his gaze intent, like he knew what she looked like beneath her clothes and he couldn't wait to see it all again.

God knew if he kept that stare up she'd bloody show him.

"Not for you." He reached behind him, pulling his phone out of his pocket. "What's your number? I'll call you with the details."

Arabella rattled it off on autopilot as he entered it into his contacts list. She couldn't quite believe she'd met a guy who knew what she looked like naked, gone for a drink with him, pashed him in a dark corner on a public street, almost invited him up to her apartment and was now giving him her number all in the space of a few hours. Normally she was much more wary with men she didn't know but hell if this didn't feel right.

He slipped his phone into his pocket, his gaze drifting to hers, his eyes roaming over her face as if he was trying to imprint her into his memory in case she disappeared again. His gaze slid to her mouth and drifted to the open collar of her crisp, white shirt. Goose bumps prickled down her chest, her nipples beading beneath the onslaught. His gaze dipped and he stared for a beat or two.

He dragged his attention back to her face, a rush of ragged air escaping his mouth, the space between them disappearing into a liquid heat. In that moment, he seemed electric, poised to act and Arabella's heart clamoured for him to do so, beating out a primal call – *do it, do it, do it.*

For one wild, pulsing, heart-stopping moment she thought he was going to take the one step that separated them and kiss her again.

But he didn't, taking a step away instead. "I'll call you," he murmured, shuffling slowly backwards.

She shivered at the silky promise. The thought of his voice in her ear fired sparks at already twitchy synapses. She was going to feel fifteen all over again, waiting for the cool boy to call her after school.

He half turned to go and Arabella took a quick, involuntary step towards him. "Be careful," she said her early fear about the dangers of his job swamping her now. "At work."

He stopped and smiled at her, nodding seriously. "I will." His voice was low but rang with sincerity.

"Aren't you worried about the dangers?"

"No."

His absolute confidence was reassuring. "Did *I* used to worry about the dangers?"

He shook his head. "You used to think what I did was sexy and exciting." He grinned. "It got you pretty hot actually."

Arabella's gaze skittered over his uniform and the way he filled it out. She took a deep, appreciative breath. Obviously nineteen-year-old Arabella had let her hormones do the talking.

His low chuckle dragged her attention back to his face. "Night," he said softly, before turning away and leaving her alone.

She slumped back against the wall for a moment or two

trying to regain her composure. Her hands shook and her legs wobbled. The stone behind her shoulder blades was comforting and solid in stark comparison to the wild flutter of her pulse.

Her phone rang, bringing her out of her stupor and she smiled as she hunted for it in her bag, knowing it was him.

The number on the screen was one she didn't recognise but she knew. "Logan?"

He didn't bother with acknowledgements. "I had a good night."

Arabella smiled stupidly into space. "Me too." She had a mountain of work to do and she doubted she'd be able to get into it after he'd kissed her into next week, but she didn't care.

"Will you dream about me?" His voice was low and sexy and her breath hitched.

"Probably."

His chuckle was deep and goose bumps feathered down the side of her neck to her collarbone and down her arm. "Will *you* dream about me?"

"I never stopped." The longing in his voice was like a finger trailing between her legs. "Good night, Bella."

Chapter Six

ARABELLA DIALLED HOME as soon as she'd made herself a cup of coffee. Her pulse was still trippy from Logan's kisses and her abdominal muscles ached from the ball of anticipation tightening in her belly. The feeling that she was waiting onboard a rocket ship about to be catapulted into the stars echoed in every breath.

Her father picked up. She'd been hoping for her mother who was less freaked out about the challenges of her amnesia than her father. He, probably most of all, even more than herself, still grappled with everything Arabella had lost. The fact he hadn't been able to protect his daughter from what had happened to her, had hit him hard.

But her mother was out so her father it was.

They chatted about the case for a few minutes before Arabella got to the point. "I met Logan Knight today."

She held her breath, unaccountably nervous. Logan had indicated earlier that her parents had known about him. Would her father pretend he didn't know Logan? And if he did – why?

There was a slight pause at the other end before her father's casual, "Oh?"

"We lived together when I was in Brisbane."

"Yes… For a while."

"Why didn't you tell me about him? Especially when you knew there was a possibility, no matter how remote, that I might run into him?"

"Logan hadn't been in your life for almost five years when you had your accident." His voice bristled with defensiveness. "Considering how overwhelming it was for you to reacquaint yourself with people who were *currently* in your life, old flames seemed a fairly low priority. And, as far as we knew, Logan didn't live in Brisbane anymore so you running into him didn't seem like any kind of possibility."

Her father had gone all lawyerly on her, his tone stiff. She loved him but that tone of voice rankled. "You didn't approve of him." It wasn't a question.

"Is that what he said?"

Arabella blinked at the prickly response. "It's more what he didn't say."

There was a long pause before her father's heavy sigh echoed down the line. "You deferred your law degree to be with him. It was impulsive and irresponsible and so very *not* you. We were concerned about his influence."

Arabella nodded. She guessed from her parent's perspective, Logan must have seemed like the anti-Christ. Luring their daughter from the path that had been laid down for her since the day she'd started in her exclusive private girl's school at the age of five.

But that was the thing, she could only *guess*. Because she had no memory of how things had gone down. A familiar frustration prickled at Arabella's skin.

"Are you going to see him again?"

Her father's voice, tense again, dragged her out of the black hole of loss. She could almost hear him holding his breath. "Yes."

He didn't say anything for long moments and it was Arabella's turn to hold her breath. How would her father handle this? *Now*? Nine years later?

He was a lawyer to the bone. Always strategising. Always exploring the options and working out the best approach. But she wasn't a client. Nor was she nineteen anymore.

"Tread carefully, darling, you're only there for three months. You don't want to break the man's heart."

He didn't say *again* but Arabella got the distinct impression that it hovered on his lips. And, as usual, her father had played his cards well. Because the last thing she wanted to do was hurt Logan. *Again.*

It had been more than obvious from their long chat that their split had hurt him. And that not remembering him – *them* – had inflicted another wound.

She'd come off four years of living through other people's disappointments where her amnesia was concerned and she'd thought she was through the other side. Did she want to start at the beginning again with Logan? Go through his grieving process with him as she had done with almost everyone she'd ever known these past four years?

Arabella didn't know if she was strong enough for that.

But she didn't know if she was strong enough to turn her back on their crazy chemistry either.

Especially if it *had* been more than just coincidence – or fate – that had put his fire station firmly on her radar.

EIGHT O'CLOCK SATURDAY morning, they were sitting under an umbrella at Simone's, inspecting the menu. Bright yellow light bathed the alfresco area and dazzled on the water. Logan had chosen the place deliberately. He hadn't been here for years but it was a popular, well-known Brisbane café and had been an old haunt of theirs.

They used to come here for breakfast after he'd finished a weekend night shift, just as they were now. She'd loved the river and the eggs Benedict and he'd loved watching the sun on her shoulders and the breeze ruffling her hair.

He'd thought a lot the last five nights. About Bella, about them, about the amnesia. He understood she was resigned to never getting her memory back but she *had* been sitting outside the firehouse that day.

A love of architecture? Maybe. Coincidence? Probably.

But who really knew what was possible? He'd been Googling the shit out of it and it seemed like no one knew definitively.

So he'd brought her to *Simone's*, to a place they'd loved and frequented hoping to shake some things loose.

"I don't think I've ever seen a menu as extensive as this," she mused as she scanned it.

Logan's heart sank. It was obvious there was nothing familiar to her here. The menu hadn't changed in over a decade – it was why people kept coming back – and she'd seemed genuinely surprised at the beautiful antique birdcages that had been turned into lights which hung from the ceiling inside the café. Lights for which Simone's was well known. Lights that Bella had always loved.

He'd told himself not to get his hopes up but he had.

"That's why the place is so popular," he said, watching her instead of the menu.

He'd been watching her for any signs of recognition but the lazy sway of her large, gold hoop earrings had been bloody distracting. Every time she moved her head they swung seductively back and forth, brushing her neck, mimicking what he'd like to do with his tongue.

She was in shorts and a tank top, the sun was on her shoulders and the breeze was ruffling her hair but it was her earrings he couldn't take his eyes off. *Christ, he must be tired.* Who knew earrings could be such a goddamn turn on?

"You're not even looking at the menu," she said, glancing at him suddenly, the hoops swinging again.

He closed the menu, crinkling his eyes against the glare.

Unlike her, he didn't have sunglasses with him. "I know what I want."

She was wearing sunglasses so he couldn't see her reaction to his blatant statement but he swore he heard a hitch in her breath. "Let me guess?" She propped her chin on her palm studying him for long drawn out moments, a smile growing on her face. "Eggs Benedict?"

"That too." He grinned.

She grinned back. "Well then." She shut her menu. "Seeing as how they come so highly recommended, I'd better get them as well."

"Good choice," he murmured as he signalled the waiter. "They also do really good coffee."

She arched an eyebrow. "I come from Melbourne. No one does coffee better than Melbourne."

Logan laughed as bittersweet memories rushed out at him. "That's one of the first things you ever said to me. Just like that, all haughty and snooty like."

"Really? Sounds very bratty of me."

"It was." He grinned despite the punch to his gut that she didn't remember something that had been seared on his brain as one of the best days of his life. "Also, hot as fuck."

Her breath *definitely* hitched this time.

~

A WAITER, WHO introduced himself as Ben, interrupted allowing Arabella to expel a breath and giving her time to gather scattered thoughts. Logan had been a mix of flirty and intense this morning and, after an absence of five days and some titillating phone conversations, she was about as turned on as she could be without her clothes catching fire.

Their orders were taken but the waiter lingered a moment or two, openly flirting with Logan about rescuing kittens from trees. Not that Arabella could blame him. Logan had come straight from work and was wearing those heavy duty navy trousers again with a plain navy T-shirt that fit snug over his shoulders. A large, white, fire services insignia was printed on the back. His hair was distractingly damp and the dark stubble on his chin and jaw was crazy sexy.

He wasn't showing any signs of having just finished five night shifts.

In fact quite the opposite.

He looked warm and fit and vital, like he could work all day and another night as well. Like he could build a house, do a thousand push-ups and slay a dragon all before eating his breakfast.

Half the women in the café had already checked him out but the fact Logan took another dude's sexual appreciation in his stride without it being some kind of personal affront only made him more attractive.

Of course, had the waiter been female, she wouldn't have felt so amused.

The waiter disappeared with their order. "Busy last

night?"

He shook his head. "A couple of jobs. A car accident on the freeway. And a trip up to the hospital."

"The hospital?"

"If the fire alarm goes off at the hospital, a couple of units have to respond to it. Even though it's usually just a nurse burning toast in a staff room somewhere. Deliberately usually."

Arabella frowned. "Deliberately?"

He nodded, a smile lighting his face and shimmering in his eyes. "It can get pretty boring in the middle of the night. Nothing like two trucks of firefighters turning up to make things interesting."

Arabella couldn't believe what she was hearing. "Do you mean they do it on purpose for the… eye candy?"

"Yes." He laughed. "It's exactly what I mean."

"So, they… objectify you."

He laughed harder. "I don't think you'll find too many of the guys objecting to being objectified. It's no hardship flirting with some cute nurses for half an hour or so."

It was on the tip of Arabella's tongue to ask him if he'd flirted with a cute nurse last night. The waiter flirting with Logan was one thing, a cute nurse was another thing entirely.

"Well, I think that's a shameful waste of resources," she said, sounding like her father now but unable to stop herself. "How much does it cost for two engines to barrel up to the hospital?"

"Oh, the service charges the hospital a few thousand dollars a pop for responding to fire alarms if it turns out to be no fire."

"And I suppose we taxpayers fork out for that? Have they never heard of the boy who cried wolf?"

Oh, for the love of God, Arabella, shut up!

She sounded like she had some kind of stake in him. Like he belonged to her. The mere thought gave her palpitations even as she was chastising herself for her uncharacteristic territorial bullshit.

"I'm sure they have." A small smile played on his mouth as he leaned forward and reached across the table, sliding his hand over the top of hers. "The difference is, we'll never not respond. It only happens a few times a year and mostly it's not intentional. Not consciously anyway. And it never hurts to practise that route anyway. It really is okay. Okay?"

"I wouldn't know," she said waspishly, withdrawing her hand. "I'm not a cute nurse."

"No, but you are a cute paralegal. Did I mention how hot even just that word makes me?"

That surprised a laugh out of her. The man sure knew how to lighten a situation. Arabella felt stupid suddenly. Here she was sitting in the glorious sunshine with a man practically every woman in the cafe – and at least one guy – would kill to be sitting with and what was she doing? Wasting time being possessed by the green-eyed monster instead of enjoying his company, basking in his easy flirting and his even easier sex appeal.

"Hot, huh?"

He nodded, a smile lighting his eyes. "I'm thinking sexy skirts and horn-rimmed glasses and going for it in a room full of musty files with you wearing one of those fancy wigs."

"I don't wear one of those wigs."

"Oh, you are in my fantasy."

Arabella laughed. The way the man said fantasy was R-rated! "*You* are a pervert."

He put a hand on his heart, completely unabashed. "Guilty as charged."

The waiter arrived with their coffees and the conversation halted. He winked at Logan as he departed and Arabella stifled a smile.

"What's been happening with you?" Logan asked as he picked up his coffee mug. "Are you any closer to putting the bad guys in jail yet?"

She shook her head noticing, not for the first time, his gaze following the motion of her gold hoop earrings and she was pleased she'd picked them. Every time they brushed her neck, his eyes followed their lazy swing and she wondered how good his mouth would feel there instead.

"It's a class action," she said, getting her head back in the conversation. "There's no jail."

"So… there's no bad guys?"

"Oh, they're pretty deplorable but they're not criminal. Not officially anyway. It's a civil matter. Negligence."

"So, what do the winners get?"

"Money. Lots of it. With any luck. They're going to need it for their medical bills. And justice."

"I'll drink to that." He raised his coffee mug. "To justice."

Arabella tapped her mug to his. "To justice."

TEN O'CLOCK ROCKED around and Arabella didn't even realise until Logan stifled a yawn.

"God. Sorry." She checked the time on her phone. "I'm keeping you up."

The slight lift of his eyebrow took her right back to the flirtiness of earlier. They'd kept to safe topics over food. Melbourne coffee. His family. Melbourne weather. Food. Hobbies. Travel. His time out west and in America. Melbourne cultural scene versus Brisbane cultural scene.

But suddenly they were back here again.

Chemistry. Attraction. Arousal.

Desire.

He looked sexy when he was tired and it ramped up his charisma one thousand percent. All she could think about was crawling naked into bed with him and twining her legs with his as she stroked his head and he went to sleep.

Of course, there were other things she could think about doing with his naked, reclined body but they could wait. He needed to sleep and she wanted to be the one he found rest with.

She wanted to be the one who kept him up into the wee, small hours too but she'd had a full five nights' sleep – first things first.

"Let's go," she said.

"I'm fine." He shook his head. "I can sleep when I'm dead."

And damn if that didn't wriggle right into her heart and set up camp. The devil made her say the next thing that left her mouth. "And what use would you be to me then?"

A slight smile curved up one side of his mouth. "Do you want to come back to mine? I have a bunch of pics I can show you from our Contiki tour."

Arabella wanted to go back to his place almost more than she wanted to keep breathing. But it had nothing to do with photos and everything to do with getting to know Logan carnally. She had no doubt that she'd end up in his bed if she went back with him.

Sure, she was interested in their past. Photographic evidence of their relationship was the kind of proof that someone like her father would crave and she'd be lying if she didn't admit to being curious about them.

But she didn't *need* it.

One look at Logan told her everything she needed to know. They had a past. He'd been seriously into her. From what he'd said, she'd been seriously into him.

And she believed him. The way her insides melted just

looking at him confirmed it. Biology didn't lie.

Based on that, staying away from him seemed wise. But the pound of her heart whenever he was near only drew her closer. God knew, she'd been unable to think of little else but him these past five days. The man was weaving his way into her consciousness and she was powerless to stop it.

She didn't want to.

After four years of hard work – physical and psychological – he looked like everything she'd been missing out on. He had mistake written all over him but she couldn't deny how much her body craved his.

How much it yearned for him.

"I'd like that very much," she said and signalled the waiter for the bill.

Chapter Seven

ARABELLA WAS SURPRISED to learn Logan lived with his brother. She'd assumed, at his age, he'd live alone although, as she was still living at home with her parents, that was hardly logical.

Maybe it was time for her to move out, too…

They drove in his Jeep to a development of old converted factories in Brisbane's Fortitude Valley. It had all the hallmarks of an inner-city area that had undergone some serious gentrification. Potholed streets and buildings covered in graffiti segueing into trendy, cafe-lined neighbourhoods for the upwardly mobile.

"This area used to be a real dive," he said, "but it's on the up now. The rent's a shocker but it's close to work as well as public transport and there're great restaurants and nightclubs nearby."

Arabella wondered how often he went to nightclubs. And did he hook up? She'd bet her last cent the man could pull. "Sounds perfect."

He grinned as he turned into a driveway. "It'll do until I

find something else."

"It was very nice of Duncan to take you in."

"I think he's just relieved to have someone to split the rent with. But it made moving back to Brisbane much easier."

Logan pulled into a car park and Arabella glanced at the building façade. Five stories of concrete painted varying shades of black and grey. "It's very… industrial."

He laughed. "Yes. The developers wanted to stay true to the history of the area and the building. They won some award for it. Grungy is the new black apparently."

Arabella got out of the car and he ushered her inside the building. They stopped at what looked like a service elevator and, when it arrived, Logan rolled the heavy door up to reveal a large inner cage structure. He pulled that door open and indicated for her to precede him before shutting both doors after them with a lot of clanging and clunking.

Ordinarily, being alone in a lift with a sexy guy who was clearly into her might well have caused Arabella's mind to turn to seduction. But not this kind of lift. There was nothing clean and bright and shiny about it. It felt far too mechanical for her liking. It reminded her she was actually in a machine.

Or possibly a *Die Hard* movie.

The lift creaked and groaned and shuddered to a halt with a huge clunk on the fifth floor and Logan repeated the process of cage opening and door rolling to let her out.

"This way," he said, smiling at her as he turned to the right and led her down a dark hallway with no ceiling, just the loom of the steel roof struts overhead.

They came to a massive steel door with graffiti and rust patches and a huge padlock. "I'm beginning to think you and your brother might be serial killers and you're luring me to your meat locker or something."

Logan laughed as he produced a key. "It's much cosier on the inside. And Duncan's on a day shift."

Which meant they were going to be all alone. Her thighs quivered in anticipation.

Arabella noticed the flex of his biceps and quads as he slid the solid metal door open on its runner. "Wow," she said, stepping inside and looking around her at the vast open area.

The internal décor was pretty much in keeping with the industrial vibe. Polished concrete floors, exposed ducting and stainless steel were the dominant features. But sunshine flooded in from the towering floor to ceiling windows, giving it a warmth and homeliness belied by the predominance of black and gunmetal grey fixtures.

"It's…big."

"Yeah." Logan grimaced slightly, as he slid the heavy door shut behind him. "Duncan's compensating for something I reckon."

She laughed and half turned to face him, sharing in the joke. He was looking more tired now but his smile lit up his face and her chest tightened. For a moment they just stood grinning at each other.

A sudden clattering noise from behind dragged her attention away from him and she turned to find a yellow Labrador, tongue lolling, floppy ears flying, barrelling towards her.

"Oh, apologies in advance for him," he said. "He won't hurt you but he might knock you flat with his enthusiasm and lick you half to death."

Arabella grinned at the dog, extending her palms to greet him as he leapt at her. "Hey, Flash." She laughed, barely containing his happy wriggling body. "Look at you, you gorgeous boy," she crooned, her hands on either side of the dog's face as he leapt around enthusiastically. "What a gorgeous boy you are."

"What did you say?"

Arabella barely heard him above the dog's happy little growls. "What?" She half laughed at the overly excited dog who had planted both paws on her chest and was now licking her face. She turned her head to look at Logan *and* avoid the tongue bathing.

He was very still, staring at her like she'd lost her mind. "You called him Flash," he said. "You remember Flash?"

She frowned. What was he talking about? "What? No, I didn't."

"Yes. You did. *Flash!*" Arabella jumped slightly at the authoritative tone in Logan's I-am-the-master voice. "*Sit!*"

Obviously well-trained, the dog obeyed instantly although, if it was possible for a dog to wriggle its ass and sit, then Flash had mastered it. His tail certainly didn't stop wagging, swishing like a feather duster along the ground.

Arabella would probably have laughed had she not been grappling with what had just occurred. *Flash?* She *had* called the dog that.

What did *that* mean? Her heart skipped a beat as a tiny flicker of excitement fluttered through her chest.

"How did you know his name?"

Her brows knotted together as she peered back into the murky recesses of her brain reaching for an answer, a memory to accompany the name. She shut her eyes, willing it to come. But there was nothing. No memory.

The flicker sputtered and died.

"*I… don't.* I don't know where that came from. I wasn't even aware I said it."

She hadn't been. Had Logan not pulled her up over it, she might still not realise.

"But… he is called Flash so *something* remembered him?"

A frustrating cloak of darkness met her mind's eye and Arabella shook her head. "No."

He took a step towards her, his tiredness emphasising his earnestness. "He was ours. He was an eight-week-old puppy when we bought him to celebrate our one month anniversary."

His words were low but Arabella could hear the streak of

desperation in them. Like if he just said it with enough conviction, she'd suddenly remember.

God. Would this nightmare never end?

"I'm sorry…" She took a step back, an ache in her chest as her heart squeezed painfully. "I don't remember."

"*Try.*"

She glared at him. God, did he think she wasn't? Her throat constricted. "I don't remember."

"Then how did you know his name?" he pressed.

"I *don't* know. Maybe you mentioned him in one of our chats?"

"No." Logan shook his head emphatically. "I haven't."

"I don't remember him, Logan," she said quietly.

Gently.

She wished she could tell him the opposite. Of all the people she'd wished that about, she felt it most acutely with him. But sadly she was used to this. To letting people down. Seeing the hope in their eyes slowly fade and die.

Feeling wretched and inadequate. Like it was her fault.

"I guess something up there fired off for me to have called him Flash but…"

"Exactly." He took a step closer, smiling encouragingly at her as if she was a toddler about to say her first word and he was silently willing her to speak. "*Something* triggered a memory."

Arabella shook her head even as her heart asked the question. What if he was right? Could it be true? After four years of nothing was it… *something?* Had the firehouse been *something*? Excitement flared again. But surely if it was there'd be more? There'd be memories to go with it? She quashed the giddy sense of possibility. She'd learned not to get her hopes up.

Been warned not to.

"No. It *wasn't* a memory, Logan."

Her voice was firm. Sure. *It had to be.* She had to make him understand. "I don't know where it came from but I can tell you I don't remember Flash."

She glanced down at the dog who actually grinned at her, tail thumping against the floorboards. He was beautiful and she had no doubt she was going to fall in love with that big doggy smile but he wasn't remotely familiar.

"He's gorgeous and I love dogs but… I look at him and I… don't remember anything about him. He's a stranger to me."

Logan flinched a little but refused to be deterred. "It has to mean something, surely? Has this kind of thing happened before?"

"No. Never." The possibility that it meant something glimmered again but the cautions from every neuro specialist she'd seen – and she'd seen many – drowned it out. They'd told her not to get her hopes up. That it was rare for memory to return once it had been taken.

An insidious thought whispered through her head. *Rare but not impossible.*

"Then maybe it means something?" he continued. "Like your memory might be starting to come back? Maybe coming to Brisbane, meeting me again is triggering it?"

Could that be true? And could she let herself hope? Let him hope? What happened if that was all there ever was? She'd chosen to let go of hope for a reason. Because she believed her doctors and hope had been too hard to maintain in the face of reality.

Hope had hurt like hell.

"Logan." The ache in her chest intensified as tears pricked at the back of her eyes. It had been a long time since her amnesia had caused her such grief. She'd thought she was used to it.

She was wrong.

She dredged up what the doctors had told her. "If it was going to come back, it would have in the beginning – the chances get less and less the more time that elapses. It's been four years and there's been *nothing*. No people or places, or events. Not even a partial memory."

"Until today."

"Please don't, Logan." She wrapped her arms around her waist trying to ward off his optimism.

Trying to protect herself from it and his inevitable disappointment. *Her* inevitable disappointment. So… she ate lunch outside the firehouse. And she'd remembered Flash's name. Two random things thrown back at her in four years? Not even *memories*.

Was it because she was here? And would there be more?

She didn't know. But she did know she couldn't live every day hoping and wishing while the swirling black abyss in her head drove her crazy with its persistent silence. Her throat clogged and her nose prickled with the pressure from absurdly stupid tears.

"You have no idea how hard this is," she said, hugging herself harder. "I'm sorry, I know you're new to all this and this is hard on you, too, but this has been *my life* for four years and its weird and surreal and took me a good while to come to terms with what the doctors were telling me but I've accepted it and I've moved on and I can't *do* this with you, too."

She hadn't cried over her lot in such a long time but she was so close over a damn dog right now it was frightening.

She glanced behind her at the huge heavy steel door. "I think maybe I should just go."

"No." He reached out a hand, expelling a long breath. It slid onto her forearm and the urge to cry intensified. "*Christ, no.* I'm sorry." His thumb stroked along the sensitive skin of her wrist. "Forget it… you're right. I shouldn't have pushed you."

"I wish I could remember," she whispered, her throat thick with emotion. "I wonder if you know how much I wish it?"

She wanted to remember everything about him. About them. About Flash. Even the dog looked suddenly forlorn and disappointed in her. Did *he* remember *her*?

A tear spilled over and slid down her face. And here she was thinking she'd done all her grieving.

Amnesia – the gift that keeps on giving.

"No, no, no," he murmured, stepping closer, his big warm body a hair's breadth from hers. "Shhh. Please don't cry." His hand slid to her neck, his thumb caressing the bony notches of her nape as his other hand found her hip then the small of her back, pressing her close, kissing her forehead. "Please don't cry. I'm sorry. I shouldn't have carried on."

Arabella shut her eyes, revelling in the solid heat of his body as he dropped light kisses along her hairline to her temple. "I've… missed you so much. I just didn't realise how much until I saw you the other day outside the firehouse. I don't want to make it hard for you."

His lips travelled to the tip of her ear and goose bumps erupted as he brushed his nose along the delicate arch. She swallowed back the sob that rose in her throat. It felt so good to be in his arms, to be held by him.

She only wished she could give him what he needed.

Arabella stood in the shelter of his body for long moments, absorbing the warmth and the strength of him before he pulled back slightly to inspect her, his hand leaving her nape to cup her jaw. His gaze travelled over her face, lingering on her mouth.

"I want to be with you. I want you to *want* to be with me. I want it to be easy."

It was crazy to want the same things on such short acquaintance but his words wove an intricate web around her, twining around her limbs and her heart.

She wanted it too.

She wanted to be with him and she wanted it to be easy but more than anything right now she wanted to kiss him. To succumb to the thrum in her blood and the desire shadowing every heartbeat.

But if anything his eyes looked more bloodshot and she could just make out the first smudge of darkness forming beneath them. It made her tired just looking at him and she'd had a full eight hours last night.

"You need to sleep," she murmured, her fingers tracing the smudges before trailing down to the slight indent in his chin. The room was silent other than the faint scratch of her fingerprints on his stubble and Flash's panting.

"Like I said earlier, I can sleep when I'm dead." His voice was a deep, sexy rumble that brushed like a physical touch up the insides of her thighs.

Arabella frowned at his choice of words, her finger roaming to the fullness of his bottom lip. Earlier, she'd joked with him about it but right now it didn't seem funny.

"Don't say that," she whispered. "I can't even bear the thought of it." She'd only just found him again.

He parted his lips at her touch. "Then come to bed with me."

Their gazes locked and her pulse fluttered madly in her

chest at what she saw in his eyes. Nothing was hidden. It was all laid bare for her to see. Naked desire, blistering passion, intense need.

He wanted her. And, God help her, she wanted him too.

Arabella pushed herself up onto her tippy toes and replaced her finger with her mouth. Soft and tentative. A shy press of her lips against his. But then he groaned and his mouth opened under hers and his arm banded around her waist hauling her in close, so close she could feel both his arousal and the hard bang of his heart.

She opened wider to him, falling into the kiss headfirst, her pulse tripping, her breathing harsh and rapid as she barely managed to keep up with the hungry demands of his mouth. He tasted like coffee and the feel of him against her filled her up until nothing else existed beyond the press and heat of his chest and groin and thighs and the delicious slide of his lips.

It was hot. And crazy. But Arabella twined her arms around his neck and anchored herself to the madness.

He pulled back suddenly, breaking the kiss, his chest heaving as he loosened her hands from his neck.

"Wha…?" She frowned at him.

"Come to bed." The dimple in his chin played peek-a-boo with his stubble as a smile flitted across his mouth.

He tugged gently on her hands as he slowly walked backwards. Arabella tried hard to coordinate her limbs and not fall down as he led her.

Flash got up to join them but Logan said, "*Stay.*"

He didn't take his eyes off her or even raise his voice but the dog obeyed immediately and Logan's tug became more insistent.

There was absolutely no question she wouldn't follow.

Chapter Eight

ARABELLA SLID HER arms around Logan's neck again as he rolled another heavy door shut behind her. But she paid no heed to the room or the bed or the décor, she only wanted his lips. And his arms.

His breath, his taste, his tongue.

His mouth.

She hunted for it, zeroing in on the ripe fullness, whimpering in triumph when she found it, the heat between them flaring like a lit fuse as they connected.

"Bella." He groaned against her mouth, her name getting lost between them as she sucked it into the kiss, rolling it around between them stoking the heat until it flamed out of control, threatening to engulf her.

Too hot for clothes. *Way too hot for clothes.*

She grabbed the back of his T-shirt and pulled, lifting it up, up, up, ignoring the smooth skin, the firm muscles, and the interesting dips of his ribcage, desperate for the feel of his skin on hers.

Needing to be closer. Needing more. Needing to know

every single inch of him.

The kiss broke apart as his shirt came off but not for long, their lips fusing again even as he yanked at her shirt and she set her hands to his fly, flicking the button open and ripping down the zip. She moaned as she dipped inside and wrapped her hand around the hard length of his cock.

"*Christ,*" he swore, sucking in a breath as he broke away, pulling her hand out of his underwear to relieve her of her shirt and, with a quick flick of his wrist, her bra too.

Her breasts had never been big but Logan looked at them like they were all day suckers, her nipples hardening as he licked his lips. Any thought she had to dip back into his underwear was lost when he tugged her close and set his mouth to one. All she was capable of at that point was arching her back and hanging on tight.

How the rest of their clothes came to be off, Arabella really had no idea. She was too far gone on the tongue-lashing he'd been dishing out to comprehend much at all. But suddenly they were both naked – even their shoes had been toed off – and his hands were on her butt cheeks and he was moving her slowly backwards, his erection, thick and heavy, trapped between their bodies.

The mattress hitting the backs of her knees roused her from her stupor. She frowned at him as he relinquished a nipple. Her breasts had patches of reddened skin where his stubble had scraped and driven her crazy.

He fingered the gold hoop in her left ear for a moment

before setting it swinging in her lobe. "Lay back," he whispered, dropping a long, sizzling kiss on her mouth. "I want to love you."

He didn't look tired anymore. He looked energised. He looked purposeful. He looked like he could love her all damn day and night.

He looked like a freaking sex god.

The pulse between her thighs kicked up a notch as she sat on the side of the bed – or slid down his body would be a more accurate description of the move, her legs wobbling like jelly. His cock jutted out long and proud right in front of her at about mouth level and she was just about to reach for him when he turned away.

His chin dimpled at her tiny mew of protest.

"Where are you going?"

"Condoms," he said.

Arabella blinked as he opened his bedside table drawer. Condoms hadn't even crossed her mind. She hoped that was more to do with her contraceptive implant than Logan's insanely good sex powers addling her senses.

Safe sex wasn't just about pregnancy for crying out loud!

She noticed some cursive script tattooed onto his left shoulder blade just as he looked over it and repeated, "Lay back."

The request rumbled from him, all low and sexy, scattering every brain cell and dissolving practically every bone in her body, making it impossible to worry about tattoos or even stay upright. She made a mental note to ask him about the tattoo later as she lowered herself down onto the mattress.

He tossed a foil packet on the pillow nearest him as he rejoined her, planting his feet firmly between hers. "God, you look sexy," he muttered, his heated gaze roving over the whisker burn he'd left on her breasts in the way only a man could.

With a look of pride and possession that melted her to the bed.

She looked sexy? The man was standing over her like he owned her, all long, tanned limbs, flat abs, and big wide shoulders. His cock jutted out over top of her thighs like it owned her. He was naked and hot and hard. *For her.*

The man *defined* sexy.

He held up his hand, palm down. "I'm nervous," he admitted, grinning as it trembled slightly and his self-deprecation was sexy as hell. Not a lot of guys would admit to that at this point of the proceedings for fear of emasculation.

Not that he appeared to be suffering from that.

He moved his hand to his chest, placing it flat over his sternum and gave a half laugh as he stared down at her. "You should feel how hard my heart is beating right now."

Arabella slid her palm to her stomach where her abdominal pulse thumped like a hammer. His gaze tracked the movement.

"If it's beating as hard as mine, we're both in trouble."

He shook his head slowly, his gaze drifting over her breasts and down her belly, lingering on the hair between her legs before returning to her face. "I never thought I'd get a second chance at a first time with you."

God. He slayed her.

Outrageously good-looking *and* a poet. Turning her on, turning her around, turning her inside out. Seducing her with his body and his gaze and his mouth.

With his lips *and* his words.

Arabella held out her hand to him. "Come here and kiss me."

He sank to his haunches, sliding his hands onto her knees, pushing them slowly apart, spreading her out before him as he shuffled in closer. Her breath hitched as his gaze zeroed in on the exposed lips of her sex. The pulse that had been beating there slowed to a thick, heavy thud as a wild tingle took over and she grew slicker beneath his gaze.

He dipped his head, his eyes firmly fixed on his target. Arabella's thighs tensed and the tingle turned to a roar of anticipation even as her brain rejected the move.

"No." Her voice was husky but the word hung firm and steady in the air between him.

Her abdominal pulse bounded harder as he halted half-way. He flicked a glance at her, their gazes locking as she shook her head.

"I want you here," she said, touching her mouth.

Did she want him to go down on her at some point? As a fully paid up, card-carrying member of the cunnilingus fan club that was a big hell, yeah. But right now she needed his mouth on her *mouth* more. God knew how many memories he had stored away of their kisses but she had none. Only the kiss from the other night, which had run on a continuous loop through her head, and the ones here today.

And it wasn't enough.

She wanted his kiss more than anything. She wanted to make new memories of his mouth moving on hers; she wanted to imprint every nuance of his kisses into her brain. Flood her grey matter with a bunch of new data.

She wanted to kiss him forever. Until their lips were numb. Until they were raw.

"I want you to kiss me and kiss me and not stop. Not even when you're inside me. Not even when you come. You have so many memories of us kissing and I don't have any." She held out her hand to him again. "Help me make some new ones."

Their gazes still locked, Logan intertwined his fingers with hers and lowered his chin to a point just above her navel where her abdominal pulse thumped like crazy. It picked up some more as her muscles contracted beneath the delicious scrape of whiskers.

"Whatever the lady wants," he murmured.

He crawled up her body, his knees straddling her thighs, as he pushed both her arms above her head shackling them there with one hand. She was completely vulnerable to him, the wicked intent in his stare liquefying her one cell at a time.

He settled on top of her, his hard dick pressed into the cradle of her pelvis. His spare hand played with the gold hoop in her ear, his fingertips brushing the side of her neck.

"Hold on, baby," he whispered, his gaze fixed on her mouth. "I'm going to kiss the fuck out of you."

And he did, his lips lowering and unleashing a torrent of kisses that left her breathless and moaning as she gave herself over to the mastery of his mouth and the hot probe of his tongue. She opened all the way for him, her mouth and her legs, inviting him closer, her pulse roaring through her ears.

"Please." She gasped for air, shifting restlessly underneath him. "I want you in me."

She needed to feel the stretch and the rock and the pound of him.

He didn't break for breath or direction, just kept kissing her as he groped for the condom. He tore it open somewhere above her head, grounding his knees and lifting his hips, reaching between them to roll it on, his mouth still fast on hers, his tongue swiping back and forth along the contours of her lips as if they were dusted in cocaine and he was an addict.

As if he never wanted to be anywhere else.

Her hands freed, Arabella clung to him. To his shoulders, to the small of his back, to the tight bunch of his ass as her pulse roared and her breath sawed and she slowly lost her mind. He was taking her apart piece by piece, deconstructing her and she surrendered to it willingly.

Then his hand was on her thigh, lifting it out and up, placing her calf on his shoulder as the blunt nudge of his cock prodded urgently against the hot, slick heat between her legs. He swallowed her cry, swooping it up with his tongue, thrusting into her mouth with the same thick urgency as his cock thrusting straight and true inside her, ploughing into her, sucking her breath away.

"Are you okay?" he asked, his breath ragged as he broke away slightly, his lips still brushing hers.

She sucked in a breath. "Yes. God, yes." Lifting her head to close the slither of light between them, claiming his mouth again, dragging them both back into the primal force between them.

It didn't take long for either of them to get to the final destination. They were in sync from the first thrust, their hot, deep, wet kisses stoking the build-up between them, tripping it into overdrive.

"*Logan.*"

She panted his name as she wrenched her mouth from his, her eyes screwed shut, her back arching, her shoulder blades dipping closer together. Had he not been on top of her she would have bowed right off the bed as every muscle in her body contracted in that moment directly before everything imploded.

"Yes, baby, yes," he muttered, rocking into her again and again, claiming her lips as she came hard and wild, moaning into his mouth and bucking in his arms.

He joined her seconds later, bellowing his own release into their kiss. She devoured it, triumphantly, her hand clamped to the back of his neck, keeping their mouths fused and their hearts aligned as their bodies threatened to launch into the stratosphere.

Even as the climax ebbed and the kisses ebbed too, losing their frenzied edge, her lips clung to his, wanting every last kiss he had to give. Even the slow, sated, lazy ones. *Especially those.* Needing to imprint them on her mouth, her skin, her brain.

Finally, their breathing almost normal, he lifted his head and smiled. He was still hard inside her, his eyes glittering with sexual satisfaction, the cleft in his chin crazy sexy. He collapsed against her, his forehead fitting into the crook of her shoulder, his lips nuzzling her neck.

"Christ," he murmured. "I think I just died and went to heaven."

Arabella smiled. Her hand was tangled in his hair and his weight, pinning her to the bed, was a delicious reminder of just how well they fit.

If this was dying then she was done with living.

LOGAN WASN'T SURE what the time was when he eventually

stirred at movement behind him. It was still bright daylight outside but the sun wasn't pouring directly through the windows so it must be well up in the sky.

He rolled over to find Bella, in his work T-shirt which sat low on her thigh – slipping back into bed.

"Sorry, I didn't mean to wake you," she whispered, sitting cross-legged, pulling the sheet up.

Logan smiled, big and slow, his heart about as full up as possible. If his eyes didn't feel the kind of gritty that always accompanied lack of sleep, he might have just thought he was dreaming.

Bella was really here. In his bed. He'd kissed her, touched her, stripped her naked.

They'd really *been* together. He'd *made love* to her.

"I'm sorry." His voice was a little rough from sleep. "I flaked out."

In the back of his mind, he'd always hoped that one day he and Bella would cross paths again. The marathon session they'd have getting reacquainted had been one of those fantasies he'd harboured late at night.

And then he'd gone and fallen asleep on her.

Actually, crashed headlong into sleep would be a better description. He vaguely recalled stumbling to the bathroom to get rid of the condom and stumbling back again but that was it.

"Are you kidding?" She shook her head at him. "You've just come off five nights. You must have been dead on your feet."

He chuckled, sliding his hand onto her thigh. "I don't think my feet were having much of a say earlier." She laughed but her breath hitched as he slid his hand a little higher. "Did you sleep?"

"For an hour or so."

"How long have you been awake for?"

"A little while."

He stroked his thumb along the flesh of her inner thigh, gratified when she squirmed a little. "You should have woken me."

"I had my phone," she said, tipping her chin at her pillow where the phone lay. "There're always emails to answer and my boss gave me a bunch of research to tackle this weekend."

Logan wanted to say *fuck research*. That he had much more interesting plans for her this weekend. But he didn't know this Bella well enough to push. The old one? She'd always been up for a weekend in bed.

"Doesn't sound like what I had in mind," he said, deliberately keeping up the lazy stroke of his thumb because her skin had broken out in goose bumps and he could hear her breath starting to roughen.

"Don't worry, I was only going to give you another hour."

"Oh, you were, were you?" He grinned. "And then what were you going to do?"

"I thought you might"—she shrugged casually—"appreciate waking up to a hot mouth on a certain part of your anatomy."

The certain piece of his anatomy in question sparked to life, appreciating it very much. "My… lips?" he asked innocently.

She smiled, shaking her head deliberately slowly, which set those big gold hoops in her ears a-swishing. "Lower."

"My chin?"

"*Much* lower."

"Ah." He nodded. "My belly button?"

She laughed. "Warmer."

Logan remembered how playful she'd always been and how he'd loved to tease her. "*Ohhhh.* My…" He let the word drift as he lowered his gaze to the part in question which was very obviously responding to the innuendo.

She looked too, her eyes widening slightly at the sight. Or maybe it was because his hand had slid higher, brushing between her legs. Her cross-legged posture gave him easy access.

No underwear – jackpot.

"Yes, your…"

She cleared her throat – maybe to rid it of its huskiness or maybe out of primness?

He laughed. "I remember you used to be embarrassed to say *that* word when I first met you," he said, trailing his fingertips against the seam of her sex.

Her breathing roughened as her eyes fluttered closed briefly. "That word?"

He nodded, a sudden rush of power making him dizzy. Not even nine years and a case of amnesia had dampened their chemistry. He could still turn her to putty. He levered himself up on his elbow and leaned in close until his mouth brushed her earlobe, the gold hoop swaying under the influence of his breath.

"*Cock,*" he whispered.

Her breath rushed out as her temple rubbed against his forehead but then her head was turning and she was seeking his lips.

"Cock," she whispered back before kissing him in a way that was so far from prim it slugged him in his balls.

It was deep and wet and dirty.

And then her phone rang.

"Leave it," he muttered, their lips brushing, his fingers growing bolder.

But she shook her head emphatically, her eyes opening. "I'm sorry, I have to get that. It'll be my boss, I was responding to an email when you woke and started distracting me."

Logan smiled against her mouth. "Cock," he murmured again but sighed as she twisted to pick up the phone then swung her legs over the side of the bed, dislodging his hand.

"Fine," he said, as she put the phone to her ear. "But you're turning that damn thing off after that."

Chapter Nine

LOGAN ROLLED ONTO his back and stared at the ceiling as Bella talked legal jargon with her boss. His eyes were still gritty as hell and if Bella wasn't here he'd shut them and probably sleep right through to tomorrow morning.

But she *was* here.

For someone who'd felt weary right down to his bones a few hours ago, Logan had never felt more alive. He glanced at his cock – a rigid outline under the sheet. It was *very much* alive.

He slipped out of bed, grabbing his underwear and stepped into it, adjusting himself to accommodate his rather inconvenient erection. He might as well power up his computer and get the photos up that Bella had, after all, come here to see. He padded over to his desk, situated to one side of the large window, sat himself down in the chair, and tapped the on button.

He glanced at Bella. She was sitting on the edge of the mattress, one leg primly crossed over the other. She held the phone to her ear in her left hand, the elbow bent and resting on her thigh as she leaned forward from her hips. His shirt had ridden up, exposing a lot of leg and it did not help his erection knowing she was bare underneath.

She didn't notice his rather lascivious gaze though, her attention fully fixed on her foot or a point on the floor near her foot. Her spare hand played idly with one gold hoop as she spoke. He didn't know why those earrings – or rather the way they swung every time she moved her head – were so sexy, they just were.

His computer beeped and he dragged his attention back to the screen clicking on the folder entitled, *Bella.* It was a folder he'd visited regularly over the years but one he hadn't been to for six months or so before she'd turned up in his life again.

He'd been through it a few days ago and removed the photos he didn't want her to see. Not before she knew about the baby anyway. They were heartbreakingly painful to look at even all this time down the track and tears had welled in his eyes as he'd transferred them to another folder. There were only a few that a nurse had taken with them and their baby but the bubble of misery she'd captured made for uncomfortable viewing.

Still, they were part of him. A part of them. Of their life. Of their story.

Bella laughed and he glanced at her as the happy sound floated to him. It needled like a splinter digging into his flesh. Keeping those photos from her, keeping that part of their story from her, didn't feel right.

Being the arbiter of what was good and bad for her didn't feel right. And if they were going to end up together again – and God knew he wanted that more right now with the smell of their sex on his skin than he ever had – did he have the right to keep something so important from her?

Still, her father's words echoed around his head. *She's happy now, Logan.* And she was. Did he have the right to take away her peace of mind just to unburden himself?

No matter the heartache, it would be far better all round for her to remember herself.

He wasn't ready yet to give up on that possibility.

The weariness he'd felt at the end of his shift slugged him straight between the eyes. He hadn't had enough sleep to grapple with any of this. Returning his attention to the screen, Logan suspected there wasn't enough sleep in the world to grapple with it.

"You have a tattoo."

Logan hadn't even realised she'd finished the call as he'd stared unseeingly at the screen. He shook himself out of his reverie and smiled at her as she headed in his direction.

Man. She wore the hell out of his T-shirt.

She drew level with him, her fingers tracing the cursive script inked on his left shoulder blade. "Brothers forged in fire," she murmured, as her cool touch streaked heat straight to his balls, his dick responding accordingly. "That's a firefighter thing?"

Logan looked up at her. "It's a Knight, thing. My grandfather used to say it all the time. *We're all brothers forged in fire, Logan.* After a few beers at his wake four of us decided to get it tattooed as a way to remember and honour the old man."

She slid her hand onto his nape, her fingers ruffling through his hair. He shifted the chair out slightly, inviting her to sit on his lap, which she did without hesitation. He slipped his arms around her waist and pulled her close. She felt good and smelled wonderful and he buried his face in her neck and just inhaled, revelling in her being back in his life.

"The investigation into the fires must be hard on your family, especially with him gone and not able to defend himself."

Any interest his cock had been showing died a quick death at the mention of the inquiry. Although, it wouldn't take much to change the situation with her ass pressing into his dick the way it was. He pulled his head back from her neck and met her gaze.

"It's been a bit of a downer for us all. It really gutted my grandfather, though. He lived and breathed the fire service. I'm not surprised he died of a sudden heart attack."

"You think there'll be any adverse findings?"

Logan shook his head. "Not in relations to my grandfather. But there were a series of things that went wrong – none of them even conceivably in his control – and I'm sure there'll be a bucketload of adverse findings over other things.

Let's hope so. Changes need to be made so that kind of loss of life never happens again."

She didn't say anything, just nodded and wrapped her arms around his shoulders, pulling him back into her. Logan went willingly, absorbing the steady thump of her heartbeat and the comfort of her body.

They sat there for long moments, wrapped up in each other before she eventually pulled away, her attention turning to the computer. "That's Croatia, right?" she said, tipping her chin at the picture on the screen. "I have one like it with a bunch of chicks."

Logan nodded, shaking off the sticky tendrils of worry. He was here with Bella and the photo was one of his favourites. The two of them laughing at the camera, arms around each other, the sun pelting down on their bare shoulders. Bella was in a white bikini, her long loose hair almost as white. He was in his boardies, tanned and relaxed.

"Yes. It's Nin."

"We look happy." She touched the screen, tracing their faces.

Logan swallowed a sudden lump thickening his throat. "That's because we were." Up until we weren't.

"Tell me about that day," she murmured, dropping her head on his shoulder.

Logan told her. About all the days in all the photos. Giving her all the information she was obviously so hungry for. Some he'd forgotten until she'd prompted him or asked a question and the details came flooding back.

How strange it must be to *not* have that ability. For a word or a question or a song or a place to not trigger a buried memory and for it to all not come back in full glorious detail.

His heart was heavy just thinking about it. Knowing that Bella didn't have that recall. Knowing that so many of her memories were based on photographic evidence instead of the real, lived experience.

Knowing he didn't exist in her brain until five days ago.

But desperately still hoping it was possible to get those memories back. That the longer she was here and the more time they spent together, the more she learned about their past, that something would give. Even something as random as the name of a dog she didn't remember.

They looked at the pictures for over an hour until he'd exhausted them all. Pictures of their whole year together, not just their holiday. Their life in Brisbane too. Photos of them with Flash as a puppy. With Logan's brothers and their friends. Pictures he'd taken of her, laughing at the camera, young and happy and in love. Selfies of them together – on the beach, out to dinner, at the top of a mountain.

Tucked up in bed together. Looking like nothing could ever tear them apart.

"Thank you," she said as he shut the folder down, adjusting her position on his lap until she was straddling him. "I loved them. I feel like you've added more pieces to the jigsaw puzzle of my life."

She slid her arms around his shoulders and pulled him close. He shut his eyes, revelling in the feel of her – the bracket of her thighs and the squash of her breasts – refusing to think about the pieces he'd withheld.

Hoping desperately she'd find them by herself.

His head tucked neatly into the crook of her neck, Logan inhaled again dragging in the essence of her – sunshine in her hair, soap on her skin, and the smell of sex.

Of him.

His shirt and his sheets.

His lips brushed the pulse that beat in her throat as he wrapped his arms around her waist. He wanted to stay like this forever, locked in the crossroads between old, happy memories and the glimmer of newer, better ones.

She stirred, loosened her arms, leaned back a little, to lock her gaze with his. "You should sleep a little more."

Logan shook his head. "I'm not tired."

"You look tired."

"Tired's for sissies. I have better things to do."

She quirked an eyebrow, a small smile playing on her pretty mouth, a wicked glint in her eyes. "Oh, really? Like what?"

"Like this," he said, leaning forward to capture her mouth.

She let him, giving in on a soft inhalation and a low moan. Sliding her arms back around him tight, opening her mouth and inviting him in, squirming forward in his lap until she was centred over his rapidly swelling cock.

He groaned as she rubbed herself against him and his hands trekked to the cheeks of her ass, breeching the hem of his shirt to clamp tight on her bare cheeks and grind himself against her.

"God." Arabella panted as her mouth broke from his, her head flopping back. She gripped his shoulders clearly getting off on the potent stimulus on her bare flesh.

The long stretch of her throat was exposed and Logan took full advantage, setting his lips to all the sensitive places, using his tongue and his teeth and his whiskers, urged on by the nonsensical noises at the back of her throat vibrating through her windpipe to his lips.

She looked gloriously sexy. The apex of her bare thighs jammed against his crotch. The T-shirt rucked up not covering much of anything south of her hips. Her neck red from his whiskers. Her chest thrust wantonly towards him because she was too turned on to even hold her head up, husky pants spilling unchecked from her parted lips.

His heart thudded slow and thick in his chest knowing that he was responsible for her arousal. Blood surged to his groin, hardening his cock to granite.

He was so goddamn turned on he could barely see straight.

"Bella," he said, groaning into her neck again, his teeth nipping at the flutter of her pulse as he flattened his palms on her ass and ground up into her hard and slow. "My T-shirt looks *good* on you. You should always wear it."

She laughed, lifting her head slowly, as if it weighed a tonne. "I'm pretty sure my boss wouldn't think it appropriate court wear."

Logan grinned. "Perhaps he's right. Perhaps you should take it off altogether."

In one smooth movement, his hands slid from her ass, up her back, taking the T-shirt with him, exposing her stomach first, then the high round peaks of her breasts.

"Oh, yes." Her nipples pebbled before his gaze. "Lay back," he murmured.

Her hands loosened from around his neck, gliding down his chest before she leaned back onto the desk on bent elbows. He didn't take the shirt off, he liked that it was rucked up high on her chest, while the rest of her nudity was completely exposed to him.

Her nipples were tight pink points, her areolas shrunken dusky discs. "Damn," he whispered, his breath hot and heavy as it escaped his lungs, his hands smoothing up her middle then diverting to either side to each flatten a breast.

"*Yessss.*"

She moaned, her back arching involuntarily, thrusting their flattened contours deeper into his hands, the hardness of her nipples scraping erotically against his palms.

"I love your breasts," he said, dragging his gaze off them to lock with hers. "I could look at them all day. I could play…" He drew his fingers up both breasts, steepling them, capturing the nipples and drawing them out as far as they'd go, loving the harsh, swift suck of her breath. "With them all day."

He let them go, brushing the tips back and forth with his thumbs. "I could suck them all day."

He dropped his head then, capturing her left nipple, drawing it deep into his mouth as he fondled the other. She cried out, bucking against him and he slipped a hand around to the middle of her back, holding her fast.

"You like?" He lifted his head, smiling at her not giving her a chance to answer before switching sides, satisfied enough by the glazed sheen to her eyes, the rough pant of her breath, the pink flush to her neck and chest.

"*Jesus.*" She moaned as his mouth claimed the opposite nipple, her head lolling back again as he used his tongue and his teeth and his whiskers to drive her wild.

His hand left her back, sliding down her stomach, two fingers slipping between her legs. Her thighs clenched and her back arched violently as she cried out.

"*Shhh, baby.*" He relinquished a nipple as he kissed up her neck to her mouth. She whimpered into the kiss as he slid the fingers inside her. "It's okay," he soothed, his thumb finding her clit. "Just lay back. Enjoy."

A string of guttural noises escaped from her throat as she broke the kiss. The fact he'd made her incoherent swelled his head *and* his heart.

It wasn't physically possible for his cock to get any more swollen.

He returned his attention to her breasts, swiping his tongue over first one nipple, then the other as his thumb teased the hard, slick nub of her clit. She was wet – so wet – the aroma of her arousal filling his head and building to a roar in his chest.

She moaned, her head lolling back again, completely surrendering to him. He took full advantage of her nearly naked and fully wanton, bared before him, bared *for him*, his T-shirt branding her as his, grazing his teeth against her nipples as he rubbed at her clit mercilessly.

"Oh, God." She gasped, her body trembling, her thighs tensing. "*Logan!*"

"Yes, baby, yes," he murmured, his chin on her sternum, watching her as he crooked his fingers inside.

She came long and hard, her face screwing into a mask of ecstasy as she clamped tight around his fingers, her pelvis bucking, her breasts jiggling as the orgasm arced through her body like an electric shock.

He kissed her all the way through it. Her chest, her neck, her shoulders, the hard, dusky tips of her breasts. Kissed her until her body had taken all it could and she begged him to stop, reaching down to wrench his hand away, grabbing his shoulders, levering herself upright, slumping against him spent and sated.

"I think you just made me forget my own name." Her

breath was warm on his neck. “Not even amnesia managed that.”

Her lips curved against his skin and he smiled.

Chapter Ten

HOURS LATER, ARABELLA still couldn't get enough of Logan's body. She might not be able to remember him but there was no denying how well they fit together.

How *good* they were together.

The light was starting to fade outside but her desire was still burning bright.

They'd spent the day in bed. Kissing and touching and talking. Getting reacquainted. And fucking. Oh, man, *the fucking*. Dozing off in between. Arabella had tried to get Logan to sleep more but he'd wake after brief naps and reach for her with such carnal intent she hadn't been able to deny him.

Or herself.

At one stage, he'd risen to grab some sustenance, bringing it back for a bed picnic. Flash had wanted to join them but Logan had shaken his head and said, "Sorry, buddy, not this time. On the couch."

"He can come in."

The door had slid shut in Flash's forlorn looking face

and Logan had shaken his head, blasting her with a look that had curled her toes. "Trust me, you do not want Flash witnessing how I intend to eat every ounce of this food off your body."

And he'd done just that starting with peanut butter, moving on to yoghurt before ending with Ice Magic – squeezing the warm chocolate sauce over her breasts and belly and finally between her legs.

They were currently listening to a playlist of Logan's through his state of the art system, the volume turned up loud. Or at least they were supposed to be but Logan's hand had wandered and Arabella had accidentally on purpose let the sheet slip a little and he'd pushed her onto her back and was kissing her into the mattress.

They didn't hear Duncan come home. They didn't hear him swear his head off at the sight of Flash getting friendly with the couch cushions.

They only vaguely heard, "*Logan!* Your damn dog is humping the cushions again." It was enough to galvanise them though and they'd managed to break apart and pull the sheets up just as the door was viscously reeled back on its runner.

"I swear to God, Logan, I–"

Duncan stopped mid-sentence as he realised Logan was not alone. "Oh. Sorry." He looked from his brother to Bella who had levered herself up on her elbows the sheet tucked firmly under her arms, to the state of the bed – strewn pillows and twisted sheets – and back to Logan again.

"Hello, Bella." He nodded awkwardly.

Bella nodded back even more awkwardly. And not just because they'd been busted and she had absolutely no clothes on under the sheet but because Logan's brother so obviously *knew* her. It was disconcerting to know that there were a whole bunch of people here in Brisbane, if those photos were anything to go by, who knew her – as *Bella* – that she didn't know from a bar of soap.

That had happened a lot in the past but she'd thought it was all over now.

She was conscious of Logan's gaze on her. She knew without him saying anything that he was watching her for any signs of recognition. The same look she'd seen on his face a few times when he'd been buried deep inside her, as if the connection alone would be enough to cure her.

But the guy in the doorway was a stranger.

"I'm Duncan. Logan's older brother."

"Dude," Logan grouched. "Do you think we can do the intros a bit later?"

Flash had joined in the fun, standing next to Duncan, wagging his tail, looking curiously at them unlike Logan's brother who was shuffling his feet and looking anywhere but at the bed. "Of course. I brought some Chinese home. There's more than enough for three." He paused. "If you're hungry."

He left then, sliding the door shut and Arabella collapsed

against the pillows. "Well… I guess there are worse things than being caught *in flagrante deltico* by the brother of the guy you've spent all day in bed with."

He grinned down at her. "I do like it when you use those big fancy Latin words. It's such a turn on."

She laughed, her hand sliding to his upper thigh under the sheet. "Coitus interruptus," she whispered. "*That's* worse."

"You're right." He pulled the sheet down and stared at her nakedness. "Where were we?"

Arabella's stomach growled. She lifted her head off the pillow and stared at it.

He cocked an eyebrow at her. "We only ate not that long ago."

Arabella's eyebrows rose. "From memory, you did most of the eating, mister."

"Oh, yeah." His smile was big and slow and lazy, a gleam sparkling in his eyes. "That's right. I didn't notice you complaining."

She grinned and shook her head. The places he'd put his tongue has erased any hunger pangs. "No complaints here."

Her stomach growled again and he sighed, dropping a kiss on her shoulder and pulling the sheet up again. "Stay here. I'll go get you some Chinese."

"No." Arabella grabbed his arm as he pushed himself up. "It's okay; we can go out and eat with your brother. It'd be rude to eat it in here with him out there."

He pulled the sheet down again and ogled her breasts. "I think Duncan would understand."

"Maybe. But"—she pulled the sheet up—"I don't fancy having honey chicken sauce in places where honey chicken sauce just shouldn't go, thank you all the same."

"Spoilsport," he murmured, pressing a lingering kiss on her mouth before she rolled away from him and sprang out of bed.

DUNCAN WAS CLEARLY surprised to see them approaching the kitchen. Arabella tried hard not to blush when she met his eyes but there was a definite trace of warmth in her cheeks.

"Did you leave us some?" Logan asked, throwing himself down on a barstool on one side of the large central bench which boasted several full plastic containers.

He stretched his arms above his head and tilted slightly from one side to the other to stretch out his lats. Arabella found it hard to think about food as her gaze followed the hypnotic movements. He was in jeans and nothing else. Not even underwear. And that was distracting as all giddyup.

Duncan pulled three plates out of the overhead cupboards and slid them onto the bench. "Help yourself."

Arabella would bet her last cent that neither of them would usually eat their takeaway off a plate but it was obviously going to be one of those times when everyone was on their best behaviour until they got to know each other a little better.

Or at least until she got to know them.

"How was work?" Logan asked his brother as he passed Arabella a plate and dragged the containers closer, inviting her to dig in.

"A house fire. A Couple of minor accidents. Pretty quiet."

They talked shop for a while for which Arabella was grateful. No input was required of her, allowing the awkwardness from earlier to ebb for both her and Duncan.

The music, which they hadn't turned off as they'd left the bedroom, suddenly changed tempo as "I Got A Feeling" from the Black Eyed Peas blared out. "Aww, this is your Bella playlist," Duncan teased, fluttering his hand over his heart. "That's cute."

Logan glared at his brother. "Duncan," he said, a warning note in his voice, which only seemed to amuse his brother more. They clearly had an easygoing relationship based on mutual ball busting.

"Bella playlist?" she asked.

"The one with the songs from your Contiki tour. God, he played this non-bloody stop when you went back to Melbourne." He laughed. "I didn't think my ears were ever going to recover."

"*Duncan*."

Arabella glanced at Logan, his face as strained as his tone, his knuckles white against the counter, his gaze avoiding hers. Had the playlist been a coincidence or was Logan hoping that it might trigger something? Like Flash had?

A squall of emotions settled in her stomach. Half of her wanted to be mad with him. But the other half wanted to cut him some slack. The man was allowed to take his time coming to terms with it and who could blame him after the Flash incident?

Despite everything, a glimmer of hope had wormed under her skin, too.

She decided to cut him some slack.

An awkward silence descended as Duncan looked from her to his brother then back to her again. "Shit… sorry. I'm not supposed to mention amnesia," he said. "I forgot."

Arabella shook her head, determined to shake off the moment and the sudden tension, too. "That's my forte," she quipped.

Duncan laughed and she noticed Logan's death grip on the bench ease, his knuckles pinking up.

"That must be some kind of head fuck."

"*Duncan*," Logan warned again, this time with more exasperation but Arabella just laughed. So many people tippy-toed around it, calling it her *condition* and talked about it being *challenging* and *taxing*.

Like it was a freaking marathon. The thing was, even marathons ended. This thing? There was no end in sight, no satisfying conclusion. She loved that Logan's brother got right to the heart of it. Amnesia *was* a total head fuck.

She leaned in closer and whispered, "You have no idea."

He grinned. "Well, I'm pleased life's brought you around this way again."

Arabella glanced at Logan. He smiled at her, relaxed again and her heart gave a funny little skip as muscles down deep and low squeezed tight.

She'd spent all day in bed with him but she already wanted him again.

She smiled back. "Me too."

Duncan rolled his eyes. "I remember when Logan first told me about you. I thought he was crazy falling so hard and fast. Talk about history repeating itself."

Arabella should be telling Duncan that it wasn't like that. They weren't young and impulsive anymore, there was a boatload of stuff to unpack between them, most of which she had no clue about and she was only here temporarily. This was just some kind of post-coital euphoria.

Except she was very much afraid Duncan was right.

"I hope we'll be seeing more of you around here?"

She dragged her gaze from Logan's to look at his brother. "I hope so too."

"Just, don't sit on any of the cushions. Logan's deviant dog has thoroughly debauched all of them in three short weeks."

Arabella laughed but made a mental note to buy more cushions. The thought pulled her up. She'd gone from hoping to redecorating in a heartbeat.

Man. She *was* falling hard.

"Hey, she should come to trivia with us on Tuesday night," Duncan said to Logan.

"Trivia?"

"At Rosie's," Duncan explained. "Every Tuesday night. A team from the firehouse always enters."

She glanced at Logan again who nodded at her and smiled, the cleft in his chin sexier than a hundred George Clooney dimples.

"I'd like that."

AS IT TURNED out, she didn't make it to the first trivia due to urgent work commitments but she made it to the next one. She barely lived at her apartment anymore having moved a suitcase of clothes and one loaded with work stuff to Logan's over the course of the week. He'd offered her the use of his computer but she had a work laptop which she used when she worked at his place.

Even the two nights Logan had been on night shift she'd spent at his place. Duncan was home and even if he hadn't been, Flash had slept on the end of the bed keeping guard as Logan had ordered him to do before disappearing out the door.

To many it would probably seem fast.

But it just felt right.

She hadn't told her parents. They always rang her on her mobile anyway so, as far as they knew, she was still at her Mary Street apartment. Although she had told them she was dating Logan again.

Her mother had said, "That's nice darling," with a strained voice and changed the subject. Her father had been even less wordy. For someone who made a profession out of being verbose, his brevity had been a big red flag.

She couldn't say exactly that they disapproved – they usually weren't reticent to express such views if they did – but she got the distinct impression they'd rather she not spend time with Logan. They just weren't courageous enough to say it.

Plus – it was none of their damn business who she dated.

They'd wrapped her in cotton wool because of what had happened to her. She understood that. But she was twenty-eight-years old. She could date whoever the hell she wanted. She might have only known Logan – again – for three weeks but she knew enough and that was what dating was all about, right?

Getting to know each other.

The fact they were also getting to know each other carnally – *very* carnally – was a bonus and absolutely nothing to do with her parents. Wanting someone like this – tearing his clothes off whenever she got the chance – wasn't either.

She couldn't wrap her head around the enormity of their sexual attraction. Even sitting opposite him in the booth at

Rosie's, sandwiched between two other people while a dude with a microphone asked questions, she wanted to drag him into the loo and blow him.

The secret little smile he kept flashing told her he knew exactly what she was thinking and he'd rather be in the loo with her blowing him too. It was exciting – heady – knowing she had this kind of sexual power over him.

Arabella glanced at him to find him watching her, watching her lips press to the rim of her wine glass, the smile on his face. Her cheeks grew warm and his smile got bigger.

The trivia host launched into his next question. "What was the name of the high court judge who resigned under a cloud of suspicion five years ago?"

"Bella," Duncan said. "Stop looking at my brother like you want to do bad things to him. This is your question."

Warm cheeks flushed to bright red as Logan threw his head back and laughed. There were six on their team tonight. Ruth Gilligan, who Arabella had liked instantly, and two other firefighters – Mick who she apparently knew from nine years ago and a rookie called Nathan who'd been on the job for ten days.

"It's okay, baby," Logan said from around the mouth of his beer bottle, his eyes twinkling. "I want to do bad things to you too."

"Oh, man," Ruth complained. "Do you mind, there are children present?" She tipped her chin at the rookie and everyone laughed.

"Come on Bella, you're a lawyer, please tell me you know this. We need a win."

Arabella laughed. "Number one, I'm *not* lawyer. I'm a *paralegal.* Number two, I did warn you having someone on your team with a nine-year hole in their memory was not a good trivia strategy. I'm amnesia girl, *remember*?"

"But you know it, right?"

Arabella rolled her eyes. "Justice Richardson. But only because I read about it recently in relation to something else I was working on for the court case."

Duncan grinned at her. "Atta girl." He was sitting beside her in the booth and threw an arm around her shoulder in a half brotherly hug, half head lock. "We're keeping you."

"To amnesia girl," Mick said, raising his beer.

Logan's family and friends had been overwhelmingly welcoming. In her honour, they'd even changed the team name to The Amnesiacs. They all raised and cheered and clinked and Arabella smiled, stupidly happy.

This trip to Brisbane was paying big dividends. She'd been hoping for a little adventure, for a change of pace but she'd never dreamed she'd make a whole bunch of new friends. Or fall in love.

Because she was falling in love.

Logan was smiling as well. He was clearly pleased that she got along with all his mates. That she fit in to this decidedly blue-collar environment despite her Toorak roots. But there was also an undercurrent of dirty in that smile.

A wicked little gleam of something in his eyes just for her.

The kind of smile that told her he wanted nothing more than to get the hell out of here and *do bad things to her*.

"We're going to win," Duncan announced as he wrote down Arabella's answer. "I can feel it in my water."

"Pfft," Ruth mocked. "The only thing you can feel in your water is the kidney stone you're making by eating all that crap food."

Everyone laughed but Duncan was right. They won that night. They won the next four weeks on the trot.

Chapter Eleven

LOGAN SHUDDERED AT the carnage on the suburban street. Both cars involved had lost control on their separate impacts. The first one had flipped over several times before slamming into a tree. The second one had mounted a gutter, hit two stationary cars in the street before ploughing into a third.

He glanced away from the screaming teenage girl who stank of booze. Her distress was emphasised by the crusted rivulets of blood down her face giving her an almost ghoulish look. Like some banshee in a horror movie.

Except she wasn't.

She was a drunk fifteen-year-old in the driver's seat of a stolen vehicle, now totally pulverised, badly pinned in while her three travelling companions lay dead, thrown around the inside of the car due to gross stupidity and a lack of seat belts.

And he had to cut her out.

Two teens from the other car, also stolen, had been ejected from their vehicle although had somehow miraculously lived. They'd been scooped up by paramedics and were being treated on scene. The driver was dead but the other passenger in the car had survived albeit in a somewhat critical condition.

His gaze fell on the real victim of this teenage stupidity. The twenty-four-year-old cyclist – a woman – who'd been struck by the first speeding car, tossed in the air into the path of the second speeding car. Witnesses, who had been out and about walking and playing and chatting with neighbours in the late afternoon on their quiet little street, said she'd landed, headfirst, driven straight into the ground. Her neck was broken, probably snapped at the instant of impact, before the second car had run straight over the top of her.

She lay lifeless under a white cellular blanket – her helmet unable to protect her neck from the spearing force of her impact. He could just make out the slight mound of her in between the legs of police who were surrounding her, talking and gathering evidence. Her mangled bicycle lay in the middle of the road where it had fallen, a police photographer taking snapshots of it.

He tried not to think about Bella – the same age as the dead woman when she too had been tossed off her bicycle. About how lucky she'd been. These last seven weeks with her had been the best of his life and he was so thankful for them.

Sure, there was no denying the nagging grief he felt over her memory loss. It had been like losing her all over again. And he still hadn't quite gotten over the brief surge of dizzying hope he'd experienced when she'd greeted Flash by name. Somewhere deep inside he longed for that. He'd lost count of the number of nights he'd gone to sleep thinking – hoping, *praying* even – maybe tomorrow she'd wake up and remember him.

Them.

That it'd all come flooding back. That she'd remember everything. Even the bad.

But, that slight mound under the blanket reminded him, it could have been much worse. That she might not have made it through her accident at all and that was what he should be thankful for.

She was still here for him to love. Whether she remembered what they'd had before or not, he'd been given a second chance with her. Even if it meant starting from scratch.

The people who lived on this typical Australian suburban street stood on their footpaths looking around them clearly in shock. Some had pulled their kids away from the horror of it all at the beginning, the others watched silently, hands over their mouths. Some even wept for the stupid young people they didn't know and for a neighbourhood that would never be the same ever again.

The street looked more like a crime scene right now. A dozen emergency vehicles – police, fire, and ambulance – were strewn along the length of it, their lights strobing into the early evening air and glittering in the broken glass that littered the road like some kind of grotesque disco.

Logan hated these scenes. He'd seen too many mangled cars and gruesome deaths. He just wanted to be home. With Bella. Instead of here, standing by while the paramedics stabilised the screaming girl before he cut her out. His gaze was constantly drawn to the unmoving shape beneath the blanket and the twisted frame of her bike and it was putting a real itch up his spine.

Give him a big nasty, vicious-sonofabitch factory fire belching black smoke and toxic chemicals and he was a happy little fireman. Attending traffic accidents like this was his least favourite thing to do. He'd rather be press ganged into inspection duties, travelling around to a variety of public venues, checking fire extinguishers and hoses and fire exits.

Hell, even school visits were preferable.

They weren't exciting parts of the job by any stretch. Not like fighting a bushfire out west or smoke jumping in Montana, but it was better than a screaming teenager and a dead woman covered by a blanket in the middle of a road somewhere.

"You're right now, Logan."

Logan nodded at the paramedics as he and two others moved in to cut the door off the car with the hydraulic rescue equipment.

The end of his shift couldn't come fast enough.

IT WAS TEN o'clock by the time he got home. Duncan was sprawled on the lounge watching tele but that wasn't who Logan needed. He needed Bella. To hold her. To bury himself in her and assure himself that she really was alright.

"How was your shift?" Duncan asked as Logan nodded at him on his way to his bedroom.

"Accident," he said, not breaking stride, not stopping to chat. "Drunk stupid kids. Four dead."

Logan didn't have to go into any detail for Duncan. Had Bella not been around, his brother would have gone and got him a beer and sat and listened to Logan rage about the total waste of human life.

But Bella *was* around and his brother knew without Logan having to say a word that *she* was all he needed right now.

She was sitting cross-legged in bed in his T-shirt, surrounded by papers, her laptop balanced on her knees. Flash dozed at the end of the bed. She glanced up with a smile as the door slid open. Flash, instantly awake, lifted his head and thumped his tail.

God, she was a sight for sore eyes.

His. She was his.

"Outside Flash," he said.

Flash obeyed immediately, padding past his master, rewarded with a quick pat.

"Are you okay?" she asked with a frown.

Logan shook his head, shutting the door behind him before striding towards her, stopping only to toe his shoes off. By the time his first knee hit the bed, she'd scooped up the papers and placed them and her laptop on the bedside table and was opening her arms to him.

He didn't say anything, just went into them, his arms circling her waist as he sprawled across the bed on his stomach, his head buried in her lap. She didn't say anything either, just stroked her hand through his hair, her fingers ruffling through the short ends at his nape, before pressing into his hairline and kneading gently.

Goose bumps skated down his neck and across his shoulders. He shivered as the sensation streaked down his spine, his glutes squeezing tight. He kissed the patch of thigh his nose was pressed against aware of her hand sliding down the furrow of his spine to the small of his back, pulling his shirt out of his waistband then drawing it up and over his head.

Logan glanced at her as she pulled it free, balancing himself on his bent elbows. He saw compassion in her blue-green gaze and concern. But she wasn't asking him for an explanation – not now. She was offering him solace.

He loved that she understood what he needed. She'd always known that, for some things, there weren't words. And finding comfort in each other's bodies was an acceptable form of communication.

His heart crashed against his ribcage suddenly feeling too big and full of emotion to be contained in his chest cavity. "I love you," he said.

It was too soon and too impulsive and just plain crazy but it was the truth – it had always been the truth. He hadn't ever stopped loving her. And his heart was fit to burst with it.

She smiled. "I love you too."

He reached for her then, awkwardly half rising to his knees as his mouth found hers, fitting against hers, pushing her backwards with the sheer force of his urgency, his hands grabbing her ass, dragging her under him as he fought to get them both horizontal.

She opened her legs and he sank into the welcoming cradle of her pelvis, her palms smoothing down his back to his ass then around the front thrusting her hands between them to grope blindly at the button and fly of his trousers as his hands pushed under the hem of her T-shirt, pushed it up, dragging her underwear down past her knees.

Her hands delved into his Calvins and pulled his cock free, palming him up and down and he groaned, breaking off the kiss. "Christ," he muttered, burying his face in her neck, his lips brushing the frantic flutter of the pulse at the base of her throat.

She guided his cock, her hands firm and sure, straight to the wet heat between her legs, notching the head at her entrance. Logan's head spun, his breath coming in short, sharp pants. He was losing all sense of time and place as the world narrowed down to just him and her in the moment.

The smell and the taste and the feel of her and the blind imperative to thrust.

She flexed her pelvis and the slick heat of her enveloped the plump head of his cock. He gasped as he looked down at her. "Condom."

"No. Just you."

Logan's heart beat a little faster. He was way too turned on to be thinking straight about this. She had a contraceptive implant and they'd talked about their clean bills of sexual health before. But…

"I want to feel just you," she said, her voice husky, her ankles locking tight around his ass.

Christ. Logan hadn't thought his heart could go any faster or feel any fuller – he was wrong. He currently didn't even know his own name but he knew he wanted that too.

Just him. Just her.

He thrust then, swallowing his groan and her gasp with his kiss, swallowing all their nonsensical utterings with his kisses as he thrust and thrust again, the slippery clamp of her around him tight and hot and perfect. He rocked into her over and over until his arms trembled and his back was slick with sweat and they were coming, hard and fast.

Stars popped and fizzed behind his closed eyes as her nails raked down his back and she chanted his name over and over and over.

THE STEADY THUMP of his heartbeat was reassuring beneath Arabella's ear. So was the solidness of his chest beneath her head, the even rise and fall of it and the warmth of his palm as it cupped the ball of her shoulder. He seemed calm and settled, all traces of their lovemaking frenzy long since oozed from his body.

And it had been *love*making. Not fucking or screwing. It wasn't anything so purely physical. Their emotions had been along for the ride. He loved her. And she loved him. And she had taken him into her body tonight to show him just how much.

She'd wanted the ultimate intimacy of no barriers between them. She'd wanted him to be closer to her than any other man. She'd wanted to express the depth and the breadth of her love in the only way she knew how.

With her body and his moving as one, nothing between them.

Something had happened to Logan tonight. She worried when he went on shift about the inherent danger of his job. Made him promise he'd be careful. He didn't look hurt but something had obviously affected him. The turmoil etched on his face had been too awful to bear. His gaze had told her he'd needed her and she'd offered him what he'd wanted – her body – and she snuggled herself closer, continuing to offer him comfort.

"What happened?" she asked into the quiet around them, the sound of the television outside a muffled murmur.

His hand tensed slightly around her shoulder and for a moment or two she was worried he was going to clam up. But then his hand relaxed and he spoke. "A car accident."

Arabella slid her hand to rest over the top of his heart, the steady thud a comforting touchstone. "Bad?"

It had to have been for Logan to have looked so devastated. She knew firefighters attended traffic accidents. She'd seen enough news footage in her life to know that. They'd probably attended hers for all she knew. But she hadn't thought about that aspect of his job or the emotional impact of it on first responders. About the effects of witnessing firsthand the kind of carnage and trauma that was regularly flashed on televised news bulletins and how dangerous it could be to mental health.

"Two stolen cars, full of drunk, joyriding teenagers. Four fatalities."

The grim news was startling. Poor Logan. No wonder he needed a bit of human comfort. "That's terrible," she murmured. "I'm so sorry."

"It was awful. But what was worse was that one of the fatalities was a twenty-four-year-old woman, an innocent bystander, riding her bicycle home from work when she was struck by the car and killed instantly."

Arabella's pulse accelerated as she glanced up his pec at him. God – that was a little close. The man would have to be a professional automaton or a sociopath not to have a human reaction to that. "And you…"

He nodded. "I just kept thinking about you. And how similar it must have been to your accident scene. How close you'd come to lying under a blanket somewhere…" He squeezed her shoulder. "And how lucky you were. I'm just so grateful that you're alive. I know you're still confronting things that your accident took from you but at least you're still here."

"I am here," she said because he looked like he wasn't and she wanted to ground him in this bed with her, bring him back from whatever was giving his face that haunted look. She turned on her stomach and propped her chin on his chest so she could look into his face, make eye contact. "I'm fine. And I'm not going anywhere. Not now that I know you love me."

The cleft in his chin winked at her as a slow smile spread over his face. He'd shaved before his shift so it was easily found and she traced the indent with her thumb as his fingers brushed a lazy pattern over her shoulder.

"Too soon?" he asked.

Arabella shook her head. "No." It was just right.

"So it's not crazy?"

"Oh, it's totally bat shit crazy." She gave a little laugh. "But…" She shrugged. "It is what it is."

He lifted his hand to brush her fringe off her forehead and Arabella shut her eyes beneath the light, drugging touch.

"It was like that the first time around too. This crazy, headlong rush into each other. I think that's our M.O."

"How long before we said it back then? And who said it first?"

"It was at the end of the Contiki tour, at Heathrow, on our way back home."

Arabella's eyebrows practically hit her hairline. "*Three weeks?*"

He grinned. "Yup. And you said it first."

It didn't sound remotely like the sensible, measured girl she'd been in high school but Arabella knew if she'd felt even an iota of what she felt now there'd be no way she could have kept it to herself.

"And then I said move to Brisbane and live with me and you said yes."

Arabella laughed and shook her head, his pec a soft pillow for her chin. "God. My parents must have *freaked.*"

His fingers momentarily stopped their lazy pattern but started up again quickly.

His grin was still there but it had slipped a bit. "They weren't thrilled. But you were resolute."

Arabella could just imagine. She might not remember a big chunk of her life but she could be determined when she put her mind to it. It had taken steel and guts to get through all her therapy, to defy the odds to talk, walk, and *live* again. "I'm impressed with myself."

He chuckled. "You should be."

She dropped a kiss on his pec, her gaze following the strong line of his jaw and the angular edge of his cheekbones.

He was sexy and she loved him and she didn't want to give this up.

Her pulse accelerated as a little more crazy took up residence in her heart. "I've been thinking…" Her finger still played with the cleft in his chin, running up and down then around his mouth then back to the cleft again. "What if I didn't go back once the court case is done? What if I stayed on here in Brisbane? With you. If"—she smiled, confident in his feelings—"you'll have me."

Chapter Twelve

LOGAN'S FINGERS STILLED on her shoulder as his gaze met Bella's. He wanted nothing more than what she was suggesting and his belly tightened just thinking about the possibilities. About her being in his life forever and always. But the spectre of what she didn't know – *what he hadn't told her* – weighed heavily on his conscience.

He slid his hand to her bare ass and squeezed. "I think I can make room for you." He smiled at her, his gaze drifting to the corresponding curve of her mouth.

"Seriously though," she said, her smile fading, her finger once again playing with his chin. "This is quick and crazy and my staid, sensible, paralegal side is telling me that I've lost my mind and that I've put you on the spot."

Logan lifted his head off the pillow and kissed her hot and hard, kissing the staid and sensible right out of her until she moaned against his lips. "You haven't put me on the spot," he said, pulling out of the kiss. "I want you to stay in Brisbane. I want us to move in together again. I want to"—he squeezed her ass again—"*have* you. Always. I'm in love with you, Bella."

She traced his mouth with her fingertip and his lips tingled. "I love you too."

He believed her. It radiated from her the same way it radiated from him. It was like a tangible force pulsing between them. He just hoped she felt the same when all their truths were out there.

He had to tell her. Everything. He knew that. If they were going to make a go of it a second time he couldn't keep such a big thing from her. Or wait around, stalling, hoping she remembered it eventually. He couldn't start a relationship with her already in a trust deficit.

She had to be told. He just didn't know how or when to do it.

She sighed. "My parents will say I'm rushing it."

Oh, she could take that to the bank.

Her father had told him he was done with interfering in Bella's life but Logan doubted he'd be cool with seeing them back together again. Especially not with Logan knowing what he knew. "I would imagine so."

"They were right, last time, according to you."

Logan nodded. "Yes, they were." The admission left a bitter taste in his mouth. He hadn't wanted to admit it at the time but they *had* rushed headlong into their relationship – moving in and falling pregnant in such rapid succession. When things fell apart, they hadn't really known each other enough to help each other through.

This time round it was going to be different. They'd spend time getting to know each other outside the bedroom. Getting to know each other's families. Working and saving for a house and a wedding and holidays. Planning pregnancies.

She laughed. "That doesn't sound like it came out easy."

Logan grinned. "Hindsight's always twenty-twenty."

"I'm not nineteen anymore," she said, tracing swirls with her fingertip over his pec. "They have to see that."

"With luck." Logan hoped so; he didn't want to be the guy who took their daughter away for the second time. He wanted to be the guy who loved their daughter.

"You said we split because we were young and impulsive and didn't fight for us."

"Yes." *And the rest.*

He wondered again if they'd still be together had it not been for the baby. He'd tried to help Bella with her grief and deal with his own but she'd kept pushing him away and he hadn't been equipped to handle it. So he'd buried himself in his work. The support of his colleagues had pulled him through that dark time but Bella had, perversely, resented the hours he'd spent at work. She'd gone from rampantly horny every time he put on his uniform to hating the sight of it.

She crooked her pinky finger at him. "Let's not do that again."

Logan couldn't agree more. He crooked his pinky and

entwined it with hers.

"I promise to fight for you, Logan Knight."

The words were light with a trace of laughter but a fierceness glowed in her eyes.

"I promise to fight for you, Arabella Tucker."

She laughed as she slipped her finger out of his, a light so bright burning in her eyes Logan fell in love all over again. "I think I should fess up to my parents. Tell them I've been living with you. That I won't be returning to Melbourne."

Logan tensed. He couldn't help but think what an eerie sense of déjà vu that was going to be for them. "Oookayyy…"

"I think if I give them some time to get used to it, they'll be more on board with the idea when the court case finishes up. I know I don't need their permission or anything but we've been through a lot together these past four years. They never left my side in hospital and were always there for me during rehab. They've been my absolute rocks. They're used to protecting me *and* having me around. It could take them a while to adjust to the fact that I'm embarking on a separate life from them and I want to handle that as gently as I can. I love them and I want them to be happy for me. Not sad or angry or worried."

"Of course."

Logan didn't object. He wanted the same things. Bella having that conversation with her parents was absolutely the right thing to do. But he was going to have to have a conversation with them too. Possibly a much harder one.

About the baby.

Because there was no way he was committing to Bella with this between them. Whether her parents liked it or not, this was going to come out.

Twenty-year-old Logan would have told Graham Tucker the way things were going to be. Twenty-nine-year-old Logan wasn't so hot headed. He was much more tempered and appreciated they were all between a rock and a hard place.

He was just going to have to convince them it was the right thing to do. Or at least give them a heads-up if he couldn't.

"I'll ring them tomorrow," she said, dropping a lingering kiss on his pec, her tongue dragging lower to circle his nipple.

Her lips were warm and her tongue was hot, a frission tunnelling under his skin from his nipple all the way down to his groin, and lower still to settle deep in his balls.

He grabbed her ass and hauled her over on top of him. She half laughed, half squealed at the sudden movement but instantly parted her legs, anchored her thighs on either side of his hips and settled herself over his burgeoning arousal.

"God you feel good just there," he muttered, lifting his head to nuzzle her neck as he clamped his hands on her ass, holding her to him as he ground himself between her legs.

"Oh, yeah?"

She pushed away slightly levering her torso off him, her breasts swaying as she flexed her pelvis, rubbing her slickness along the granite hard length of him. "Prove it."

He grinned. "My pleasure."

Then he rolled her over in one swift, easy movement, pressed her into the bed, and took her breath away.

~

ARABELLA DIDN'T RING her parents the next day. Or the day after that. She waited until she was walking to Rosie's after work the third day before she rang. To be fair, it had been crazy at work. Early starts, late finishes, and snatched lunch breaks. But she *could* have carved out time to talk to them had she been motivated enough.

And therein lay the problem. She knew what she had to do. What the right thing – the responsible thing – was. But there was something nice about this honeymoon period. Knowing Logan loved her, that she was going to stay on here in Brisbane to be with him, that they'd find a place together just her and him. And Flash.

It was like they had a secret between them that was delicious and illicit and *theirs*. No one else knew about it – not even Duncan. Which meant no one could judge.

Or condemn.

The tension in Logan's body whenever she mentioned her parents was enough to keep her putting off the inevitable phone call. Clearly, he'd already had a brush with them at their most intimidating. She could only imagine how much they'd disapproved of him when he'd lured their nineteen-year-old daughter away from not just them but her studies.

But neither of them were those young irresponsible kids anymore. And it was time to act it and get everything out in the open.

Her throat was as parched as a burnt paddock as she waited for them to pick up. It would be just after seven in the evening in Melbourne and they'd be finishing their evening meal by now – probably enjoying a glass of wine in front of the news.

Her parents were creatures of habit but also busy lawyers who had been trained early to never ignore a ringing phone.

Arabella's pulse beat loud in her ears and she licked dry lips. She shouldn't be nervous. These were her parents for crying out loud. The two people who, apart from Logan, loved her most in the whole world. Who wanted her to be happy and settled and fulfilled.

But it was also why the stakes were so high. She wanted them to *like* Logan. She needed them to like him. She didn't want to be forced to choose between them. Clearly nineteen-year-old Arabella had chosen Logan over them but *this* Arabella wanted them both in her life.

"Mum?" she said as the familiar voice answered the phone.

"Arabella!"

Tears pricked at the genuine warmth in her mother's

voice. She missed her with a sudden fierce rush. Her mother had always been her greatest advocate but never more so than when she'd been recovering from her injuries and too many decisions had seemed overwhelming.

"Darling, it's Arabella," her mother called to her father. "Hang on; I'll put you on speaker."

They chatted amiably for a few minutes about the case that looked like it was going to wrap up in about three weeks and they told her about all the goings on at the office and the renovations that were underway to make more efficient use of the space.

"Oh, that reminds me," her mother said. "Charles was saying that when you get back, he wants to move all the paralegals to the opposite end of the building."

It was as good an opening as any. "Actually I kinda wanted to talk to you about that."

"About moving to the other end?" There was a frown in her mother's voice.

"No. About after. When the case is done."

"Yes?" It was her father this time, his lawyer voice half wary, half stern. "What about *after*?"

Arabella took a steadying breath. "I'm not coming back to Melbourne. I'm going to stay on here."

There was silence. It went on for an uncomfortably long period of time and Arabella's palm where she held the phone was actually sweating. "Mum? Dad?"

"Arabella, I…"

Her mother's faint voice faded off to be quickly replaced by her father's in full barrister mode. "This because of Logan?"

"Yes. I'm in love with him."

"You've known him for less than *three months*, Arabella," he said, his voice scathingly dismissive.

"I've known him for *much longer* than that and you know it, Dad."

He didn't seem to have a comeback and Arabella was pettily pleased she'd shamed him into silence. If only it would last.

"But darling…" Her mother again, her voice stronger. "Your life is here. Your family and your friends. Your job."

"I'll get another job, Mum. And I'll make new friends. And there're these things called aeroplanes. Melbourne is a two-hour flight. I'll come home to visit. And I hope you'll come here to visit me."

"We don't have time to go traipsing around the countryside *visiting*," her father snapped. "We're running a law firm."

"Maybe you should come home for a few weeks first?" She was calmer than her father but a thick edge of worry was clearly audible. "There'll be things to settle here and it might help you to be sure you're making the right decision. To know what you're giving up. Don't rush into it, darling. Maybe stay in Melbourne until you can secure a job in Brisbane and we've found a replacement for you."

"Yes, damn it," her father said, "you can't just leave us in the lurch like this. I will *not* accept your resignation." Arabella held on tight to the phone and her patience. The law firm had a pool of paralegals. They'd hardly miss one. They'd made do without for the class action for crying out loud.

"I'm not in your court room, Dad, so please don't treat me like I am." She kept her voice calm because she'd seen her father railroad people before and she was determined she wasn't going to be one of them. "I'm not ringing to ask your permission. I'm just letting you know that I'm not coming home. I don't want it to be like it was the last time with Logan."

"You don't know how it was last time," he said, his voice an angry hiss down the line.

Arabella reared back as if her father had slapped her. He couldn't have hurt her anymore had he *actually* slapped her.

"Graham, please…" her mother said quietly.

"No," Arabella said, emotion clogging her throat, "you're right. I don't know. Only what Logan's filled in."

A disgusted snort filled her ear. "If he's told you that we–"

"*No!*" Arabella was done listening to her father.

Logan hadn't said one bad thing about her parents even though she *knew* from the tension that crept into him whenever she mentioned them they'd made things difficult for him. Or her father had anyway.

"He hasn't told me a *damn* thing about what happened between you guys. He doesn't *need* to. His silence is telling enough."

A thick hush, crackling with tension, flowed through the airwaves between Brisbane and Melbourne. She could hear her father's short, sharp breathing and the low unintelligible murmur of her mother's voice as if she was trying to soothe him.

"We just… worry about you darling," she said eventually.

Arabella sighed. She understood why her parents still felt so protective of her. But it didn't make it any less chafing. "I'm fine, Mum. You don't have to worry about me anymore. I'm happy. *He* makes me happy."

There was a sound that sounded suspiciously like a muffled sob, then, "That's all we ever wanted for you."

Arabella knew that was true. That all her parents wanted for her and for her brother and sister was for them to be happy. But their definition of happiness was not the same as hers. For them, happiness was prescriptive. The right job, the right city, the right university, the right people, the right friends, the right partners.

She hadn't really thought about happiness since her accident. *True* happiness. Because, of course, she *had* been happy in Melbourne with her job and her friends and her family. But knowing what she knew now about her prior relationship with Logan, about her nineteen-year-old self breaking away from all that prescription to be with him, she knew she mustn't have always subscribed to their brand of happiness.

That she must have found a different kind.

A better kind.

Maybe it was just the naivety of a nineteen-year-old but, maybe, that nineteen-year-old had been wise beyond her years.

Chapter Thirteen

LOGAN DIDN'T GET a chance to ring Bella's father the next day and talk to him about Bella coming to live in Brisbane.

Graham Tucker rang him.

Bella had told him about the phone call with her parents and he'd planned to ring Graham on his lunch break but his phone rang at nine on the dot and he recognised the number from when he'd rung the law firm all those weeks ago.

"Graham," he said as he tapped the answer button on the screen, mentally preparing himself for whatever the hell was about to unfold.

"I hear you make my daughter *happy*."

Graham made happy sound like a particularly virulent form of herpes and Logan felt absurdly like laughing.

He didn't. "She makes me happy too."

The short silence that followed left Logan in no doubt that Bella's father didn't give one fuck for his happiness.

"She seems determined to turn her back on everything she knows and loves to move three thousand kilometres away."

Logan shut himself away in an office. Privacy around the station was impossible. "She's moving to Brisbane. Not the moon."

"She's rewinding nine years of her life, that's what she's doing."

"She's not nineteen anymore, Graham."

"And, yet, still as impulsive."

"I thought you weren't interested in controlling her life these days?"

"I'm not. But I want her to make *considered* decisions, not rash, reckless ones as befitting her *not* nineteen-year-old self."

Logan sighed. He supposed, no matter his age, he was always going to be some punk who was taking away Graham's daughter and, maybe, no matter what he did, the old man would never forgive him for it.

"Look, I'm sorry." And he was. To a point. He could sympathise with Bella's father much more than he used to. "I know this must be some horrible kind of déjà vu for you but–"

"Why be sorry?" Graham interrupted, his voice dripping with sarcasm. "You won."

"*Jesus,* Graham." Logan ran his hand over his short hair. "This isn't a competition."

That seemed to shut him up and for long moments neither of them said anything.

"You're going to tell her about the baby, aren't you?"

The weariness and worry in Graham's voice was more potent than his sarcasm or his anger. Logan closed his eyes briefly.

"I have to."

"And what if it destroys her all over again?" Graham demanded, not bothering to disguise his anguish. "Are you prepared for that? Are you prepared for what it could potentially do to her?"

No. He wasn't. Logan dreaded it. The potential consequences of telling her about the baby had played in his head repeatedly for weeks and he hated that Graham could be right. That it could have an adverse effect. On her mental health. On their fledgling reunion.

He wished he didn't *have* to tell her but secrets like this had a nasty way of coming out in the end with potentially much worse consequences. What if one day she did get her memory back? How would she take it, knowing he'd been lying to her by omission for years? He was between a rock and a hard place, as her parents had been and it pissed him off enough to lash out.

"You're just worried about covering your own ass. You know it was wrong to keep this from her and you know she's going to hate you for it."

"Well, I'm not going to be the only one, am I?" Graham said. "In case it's escaped your notice, you've been keeping this from her too."

"Because of *you*, damn it," Logan snapped. "The only reason I haven't told her yet is because you practically begged me not to."

"Yes. As I'm doing again."

"God… Graham…" Logan shook his head. This *sucked*. "I *have* to tell her. I can't go into a relationship with her keeping this from her. Lying to her like that. She had a baby. A little girl. *Your granddaughter*. She *died*. Now, I know I'm not your pick for Bella but this *happened*. It's too big to keep to myself. And you know these things have a way of coming out. She has a *right* to know this. It's her *medical* history. For fuck's sake, Graham, you're a lawyer, you should know that."

A long sigh sounded in his ear. "I just don't want to see her hurt all over again. She's already been through so much."

"Do you think *I* do?" Logan asked, his voice low, anger and tension seeping from his shoulders at the sincerity in Graham's voice.

A lengthy pause. "No."

"I *love* her."

"So do I."

The phone went dead in his ear and Logan stared at it for long moments. Once upon a time, he'd have thought the love between a woman and a man trumped all other kinds. Now he was old enough to know it was just different. Not more or less. Different. And he really did feel for Bella's parents. Hell, he even understood why they hadn't told her.

But that didn't mean he had to like the situation they'd

put him in.

I can handle the truth.

That was what she'd told him that first day at Rosie's. He hoped she was right because he couldn't put off telling her any longer.

For better or worse, he was going to speak to her tonight.

LOGAN GOT HOME at eight, dread as deep and dark as a mine pit in his belly. His pulse picked up as he neared the apartment door, his hand shook as he inserted the key.

Bella wasn't in the lounge, neither was Flash. But a slice of light shone from his open bedroom door and low music drifted out. He took a deep breath and made his way over.

The sight of her pulled him up in the doorway. Sitting on his bed surrounded by papers, in one of his old T-shirts, her legs akimbo and mostly exposed, a dozing Flash using one of her feet as a pillow. She was tapping away at her laptop, placed on the bed in the space between her thighs, a frown of concentration crinkling her brows, a pen gripped horizontally between her teeth.

He grinned at the scene despite his heavy heart. If it all ended tonight, this would be the way he wanted to remember her. He pulled his phone from his back pocket and snapped a couple of quick pics. Flash heard the shutter noise a fraction before she did and lifted his head, immediately wagging his tail.

She dragged her gaze off the screen and glanced at him, a big smile breaking over her face as she removed the pen from her teeth. It was like a sledgehammer to his heart.

"God, you look hot in your uniform." Her gaze travelled over him very thoroughly, heating his blood.

"You look hot in my T-shirt."

"You really should come over here and do me."

Logan laughed, snapping a couple more pics as he walked towards her. "Don't." She held up her hand in front of her face. "I'm not wearing any makeup. Or a bra."

He crawled onto the bed, paying no heed to the legal papers crunching under his knees. "Oh yeah," he said, pulling the yoke of the shirt out and looking down at her deliciously bare breasts, the pale pink nipples hardening before his eyes.

His cock followed suit.

"You're right." He tutted and snapped a pic down her shirt.

"Hey." She laughed around his kiss, pulling out of it way too quickly for his liking. "Give me that phone right now. I'm deleting that."

Logan kissed her again but handed over his phone. "I'm going to take a quick shower. To be continued."

If he stayed, he'd have her under him in a blink and he couldn't make love to her without talking to her first. It felt too dishonest.

But he wasn't above putting off the inevitable either.

ARABELLA DELETED THE pic of her breasts and edited a couple of the other ones he'd taken that were quite good. On a streak of naughtiness she pulled the T-shirt up and posed, bare-boobed for a pic. This was better than the other one. For a start it was more than just a pair of boobs as she pouted at the camera and thrust out her chest.

The dog, whose head was back on her foot, blinked at her as she bared her wares. "Sorry Flash," she said on a half laugh, pulling the T-shirt down. He flopped his head to one side like his doggy brain couldn't quite comprehend what he'd just seen.

Quickly, she navigated to the folders in Logan's camera setting. She didn't want the picture to be just there for anyone to see. Or him either. She wanted to hide it a little so it was something he'd stumble upon one day when he least expected it.

She smiled to herself thinking about that moment. Thinking about the double take then that secret, dirty smile of his spreading across his mouth.

Arabella started to make a folder but saw there was already one made called *Bella.* Perfect! She opened it to add the new pic but got distracted by the other pictures. There were a lot from the last couple of months and she smiled at the memories. She'd seen a lot of the others on Logan's computer that day he'd shown her the Contiki snaps.

There was one she hadn't seen, though.

One that froze her to the spot.

Her and Logan. Not looking young and happy and in love. Not grinning or kissing or mucking around. Not even looking at the camera. Looking down at a bundle in her arms.

It was a baby. A very small, very lifeless looking baby. Arabella could see a head and a tiny, tiny grey hand she held in her own. She was in a hospital bed, her name on the backboard, a blood pressure cuff around her arm, a drip in the back of her hand.

Logan was crying. So was she.

The abject misery on their faces chilled her to the bone. Bella's heart thudded painfully in her chest as her brain tried to reconcile the image she was seeing.

Was that *their* baby? Had she been *pregnant?*

Had she had a baby?

Involuntarily, her hand slid to her stomach. *She'd had a baby*?

No. She'd *lost* a baby.

"Man, that feels better."

Bella glanced up from the phone to find Logan grinning, walking toward her, a towel slung low on his hips. It didn't have its usual effect. Her face was frozen, her brain uncomprehending as the discovery played like an old cracked record in her head.

A baby. A baby. A baby.

She didn't know what she looked like but it must have

been bad as Logan's step faltered and his grin faded.

"Bella?" His voice seemed to come from a very long way away even though he was now standing at the foot of the bed.

"What's this?" On autopilot, she turned the phone around in her shaking hand.

His eyes fluttered shut briefly and Arabella knew in that moment this wasn't some sick joke or some weird anecdote that Logan could just explain away. That there wasn't some easy answer.

He opened his eyes, the grey of his irises smoky with anguish. "That's our daughter, Faith. She was stillborn at twenty-two weeks."

Arabella gasped, shocked by the admission, unprepared for his honesty. She'd been desperately hoping it wasn't what it appeared. She looked at the picture again.

She'd had a baby.

It was too hard to wrap her head around. Too… *big.*

Her skin crawled, like a thousand ants were marching just under the surface, like it had been set alight. She dropped the phone and scrambled off the bed, pacing to the desk and back, unable to sit still, scrubbing at her arms to stop the mad, tingling of her skin.

"Bella?"

She ignored him and paced some more. Her brain going round and round. She'd had a baby girl.

Faith.

How could she *not* remember that? How could *anything* erase *that*?

"Bella."

She pulled up short and stared at him. He was standing at the end of the bed still, looking helpless and worried.

"I was pregnant?"

"Yes. It was an accident but… after the initial shock, we were excited about it."

"I don't remember," she said, hugging her arms around her waist.

He nodded. "I know."

"I *don't* remember." It was louder this time. More demanding. More accusatory.

"I know."

She paced again, finding it harder and harder to breathe around the block of ice growing in her chest. Just when she'd thought amnesia had delivered its final surprise with meeting Logan, it still wasn't finished with her.

She'd given birth to a baby and she didn't remember.

She *didn't* remember.

She stopped by the desk chair and hung onto the back. The injustice tore at her heart and sucked away her breath.

"Why?" she demanded, whirling around to face him. "Why didn't you tell me?"

What the hell had he been playing at? Didn't he know she'd want to know *that*?

"I'm sorry… I was going to tell you tonight."

A sudden, blinding flash of white-hot fury seared her nerve endings. "*Tonight?*" she yelled. "Tonight? You should have told me at the beginning. *Why?*" she demanded. "Why didn't you tell me straight away?"

He took a step towards her. "I wanted to but–" He stopped.

She waited for him to keep going but he shook his head as if he was grappling with something.

"I should have," he said finally.

Arabella narrowed her eyes. She hadn't spent years in courtrooms without being able to tell when someone was obfuscating. "You wanted to but *what*?" she said, her voice low and silky with anger. "Do not piss me around on this, Logan."

He took a breath. "Your father asked me not to."

"My... *father?*"

She blinked, confused. *Her father?*

Of course, her parents probably knew about it. *And they hadn't said anything either.* In fact, it sounded very much like her father and Logan had... colluded over keeping it secret?

"I'm sorry... Have you been talking to my father, behind my back?"

He nodded, looking miserable, like he'd rather be anywhere but here right now. "I rang him that day we first met. To ask him about the amnesia. To... demand to know why they hadn't told me about your accident. To check what you knew and what you didn't. That's when he asked me to not say anything about the baby."

"And you just… *did what he asked*?"

Arabella had gotten the distinct impression there was no love lost between her father and Logan and yet Logan had agreed to something so wildly unfair to her?

"Yes." Logan sighed. "I argued against it. I didn't agree with it but… yes. Initially anyway."

"*Why*?" she demanded, dashing away a tear that was trekking down her face. She didn't even know she was crying. "I thought you loved me? *Why*?"

"I *do* love you, Bella but… he was afraid *this* would happen. It was… rough… afterwards. For you. Well… for both of us but… your grief was…" He broke off, shaking his head as if he didn't have the words for it.

"Was what?" she asked, hugging herself again, *needing* to know. *Because she couldn't remember.*

How had she grieved for a baby she didn't remember?

"It was… deep and dark and I was… so *worried* and…" He rubbed a hand over his hair. "Inadequate. I didn't know what to do."

Arabella could tell by the devastation on his face and the way he was choosing his words that he was leaving a lot unsaid. It sounded like she'd been a real mess.

"Is that why we split? You said when it came to the crunch we didn't fight for each other. You mean *I* didn't fight for us?"

"No." He shook his head, taking another step towards

her, their gazes locking. "*No*, Bella. It takes two people to make a relationship breakdown. And we were both young and we barely knew each other and suddenly we were dealing with an unplanned pregnancy then a stillbirth and a *shit tonne* of grief and we didn't have the skills or enough history together to cope with it all. It was just a *really* shitty time and your parents came for you and you wanted your mother and… I let you go."

The ache in his voice twisted inside her gut. The emotions from that time were clearly still as raw as ever for Logan. No wonder he'd been so devastated when they'd first met again and he'd realised she didn't remember any of what they'd been through. That those memories weren't reciprocated by the one person in the world who'd been through every miserable one of them with him.

No wonder he'd kept looking at her with hope in his eyes. Like maybe she'd suddenly remember it all. Because how could anyone forget such a devastating experience?

"You let me go?"

God, how hard must that have been for him? If he'd loved her as much then as he did now? While trying to cope with his grief, too?

"Yes. For a month. And then I went to Melbourne to bring you back. But…" He dropped his gaze, looking at his feet.

She nodded, knowing without knowing how it had gone down. "I rejected you."

"Yes." He glanced up swiftly, hope in his eyes as he searched her face for signs of the same memory.

His slow dawning that it had just been an educated guess was hard to watch. His raw expression told her what she'd been trying to ignore. That he was still holding out hope where her memory was concerned.

God…

She couldn't deal with this. Not with this startling information. Not with his expectations. Or his disappointment. Or his grief-stricken memories written plain across his face. Or her parent's complicity.

It was too, *too* much.

There were so many questions tumbling around in her head about the baby. She wanted to know it all – every detail – but it was too big to fit inside her at the moment. Her heart hurt and her head was spinning and her lungs felt like they were going to burst out of her chest.

It was too much to take in.

And his face was destroying her. His sexy, stubbly face, twisted in despair and sorrow. She was too mad with him right now to empathise.

She'd had a *baby* with him and he'd kept it from her. The knowledge had been lost to her and *he'd* chosen to keep it that way. To withhold it. She'd bared her body and her soul to him. She'd given him everything – she'd fallen in love with him all over again, she was staying here with him – and he'd been holding back.

She felt… *betrayed.* By someone who was supposed to *love* her.

Still… she felt an insane urge to apologise. For what she didn't know. A bubble of hysteria rose in her throat and she swallowed it down. For losing his baby? For her deep, dark grief? For rejecting him.

All those things that she *didn't fucking remember!*

He did though. And that was the clincher. He knew everything and she only knew the bits he'd deigned to tell her. And right now, she couldn't deal with that.

Arabella stepped back one step, two, then turned away, striding to the cupboard, pulling shorts out of the draws and hastily stepping into them.

"Bella."

She ignored him, whisking his T-shirt off and pulling on one of hers, not bothering with a bra. She shoved her feet into a pair of flip flops, glad she still had a lot of her clothes at the apartment.

"Bella, please don't go."

She turned for the bed, grabbed her laptop and shoved it into its bag. She gathered all the papers and shoved them in too. She picked her bag up off the floor and her phone. Her movements were calm and measured, reflecting the iciness that was spreading from her core to all her peripheries.

"Don't walk out again," he said as she faced him. "Stay and fight for us this time."

His words found their mark. "Screw you, Logan. You

didn't fight for *me*, for my right to know."

"I'm so, *so* sorry."

She believed him, for what it was worth. But that didn't stop how much she was hurting. "I can't be here, right now."

He nodded, the yearning for her to stay was clear in his tortured, grey gaze, but he was ultimately resigned. "Okay."

Arabella headed for the door, stopping to pat Flash briefly before continuing. She was going to miss him. And his master.

"I'll call you tomorrow," he said before she disappeared out the door.

She halted but didn't turn to face him. "Don't. I'll call you. When I'm ready."

And she walked out of the apartment.

Chapter Fourteen

ARABELLA WAITED UNTIL she got to her apartment before she rang her parents. She didn't think the Uber driver wanted to hear her rant or ugly snot cry and she needed time to cool down and order her thoughts.

She hadn't cooled down by the time she dialled their number but she was thinking a little clearer.

"I had a *baby*?" she said, her voice terse, not bothering to find out who'd picked up before launching into it. "I was pregnant and had a baby?"

"Logan told you." It was her father.

"No," she snapped. "I found a picture. And *then* he told me the whole damn *conspiracy!*"

"Now, Arabella." Her father's tone was irritatingly condescending. His court voice.

"Don't you *now Arabella,* me!" she yelled. Her hands were shaking – hard. "Why on earth would you *keep* that from me?"

"Darling…" Her mother this time. He must have put it on speaker. "It wasn't… intentional. But we should have told you. We're so, so sorry."

Arabella laughed a harsh, snorting noise. "Yeah. It seems like everybody is *sorry.*"

"We didn't plan to keep it from you," her father said, more contrite now. "It just happened."

"So you didn't sit down and discuss whether to tell me or not."

He sighed. "Not… in the beginning."

"Right. But you *did.* At some point."

"Those first weeks and months we were just concentrating on getting you better and getting you home, darling," her mother said. "That was all we could really think about. And then there was your lengthy rehab and it took you a long while to even *want* to fill in those memory blanks. And the doctors told us to be guided by you, not to push, to wait for when you were ready to know things."

"But you could have told me when I found out I'd lived in Brisbane for a year. You could have told me about Logan. And the baby."

"We could have but…" It was unusual to hear even a whiff of hesitancy in her father's voice. "You have to understand. We had our old Arabella back. After you lost the baby and had come home… you went into a terrible depression. For over a year. We got you therapy and you were on medication but nothing seemed to be able to pull you back from your grief. The bubbly, bright Arabella everyone knew and loved was …gone. We were at our wit's end. I would have done *anything*, given *anything*, paid *any* money to have erased your pain. But there was nothing we could do."

Arabella could hear her father's anguish but felt oddly detached from it. From him and this strange story of *her* life. It confirmed what Logan had said about her mental state after she'd lost the baby but her father could have been talking about a stranger.

"You *eventually* got better. You functioned again. You went back to law school, you re-entered society but you were never the same. There was a sadness about you that was haunting. And then you had your accident and the entire thing was magically erased from your memory and we had our old Arabella back. It was the *one* good thing that had come out of your accident."

"And the longer we went without telling you the harder it was to tell you." Her mother's voice was shaky as if she was on the verge of tears. "To find the right moment. And we didn't know how you'd react to the news. We didn't want to take you back to that dark time again, sweetheart. Or risk plunging you into despair again. Having you hurting all over again. We just… couldn't. But it was wrong. It wasn't our secret to keep."

"It wasn't Logan's either," she said. A well of anger rose at their complicity, refusing to be quelled.

"Don't blame him," her father said, surprisingly quick. "There wasn't some kind of conspiracy. He wanted to tell you right away and he didn't because I asked him not to."

"Oh, I'm *not* blaming him," she said, knowing her father was damn good at reading in between the lines. She was laying the blame for Logan's collusion squarely at her father's feet. "But I am *angry* at him for agreeing. Why did you ask him to do that?"

"Because you were only going to be in Brisbane for a few months." Her father's logic was obvious to him but not so much to Arabella. "You were supposed to be coming back home to your life. What possible purpose could it have fulfilled for Logan to tell you? To possibly devastate you? We didn't know that you were going to fall in love with him again."

Why? The question poked its way into her brain. Why didn't they know that? Did they think her amnesia had reset her hormones? Why *wouldn't* she fall in love with him again? She was beginning to think that some love transcended things like time and memory. That some people were destined to connect, to be together.

How else did she explain Logan and her meeting and falling in love *twice*?

"So you were just… going to keep this from me? *Forever?*"

"Darling… no. We hadn't really–"

"Yes." Even from three thousand kilometres away, Arabella could hear her mother's conflict but her father's abrupt honesty as he cut in held no conflict whatsoever. "If at all possible *yes*. I'm sorry if that's not what you want to hear."

She shook her head, a tear squeezed out of her eye and trekked down her face. “That’s not your call, Dad.”

“I know it’s not, *damn it*,” he said, sounding both annoyed and righteous. “But I’m supposed to protect you from being hurt. I couldn’t protect you the first time around and it ripped our hearts out, watching you go through such terrible mental anguish but I could this time so, yes… damn it.”

“I’m not a child,” Arabella chided.

The accident had rendered her helpless for a long time and her parents had coddled her and she’d let them because she’d depended so heavily on them. But she was better now. She was well. She was a grown ass woman looking after herself.

“There comes a time when every person has to stand on their own two feet,” she said. “I’m twenty-eight, I don’t need your protection. I need your honesty.”

“Right,” he said, in his court voice. “And how do you feel now, Arabella? Now that you know?” he demanded. “You feel *better* for knowing? You feel *happy*. You feel good about yourself? Or are you going to crawl under the covers of your bed and cry yourself to sleep? Not talk or eat or work or *live*? Just be consumed by it? Like last time?”

A hot ball of hurt exploded the ice in her chest, flinging a million icy shards like tiny needles everywhere.

He didn’t get some kind of absolution from her because he was trying to protect her from some potential emotional fallout.

"I'm *angry,* Daddy."

It had been a long time since she'd called her father Daddy. *That was* how pissed off she was. It boiled in her bloodstream and streaked like forks of hissing lightning up and down her spine.

"I'm *really* angry at you two for keeping this from me. I'm *angry* at Logan for doing the same. But I'm *not* going to fall apart. How could I?" she yelled. "*I. Don't. Remember.*"

She hung up the phone, wishing it was one of those old-fashioned corded ones so she had the satisfaction of banging it down. It rang almost immediately. *Home.* She declined the call. It rang again. *Logan.* She switched it off.

She was too angry with either of them to talk.

She lay on the bed instead, tucking her legs up until she was as small as she could be. Her chest burned from the pent-up emotions she'd been trying to keep at bay as her hands slipped to her belly. She cradled it, trying to wrap her head around the fact that once upon a time, a life had grown inside her.

For twenty-two weeks.

Logan's baby. A little girl.

Arabella waited. And waited. Lying there, hoping she'd get some kind of sense of that life. A feeling that, if only for a brief moment in time, she'd been a mother. She squeezed her eyes shut, peering into the black hole inside her head where the memories were locked in some kind of abyss, frustratingly out of her reach. She peered so hard it felt as if her skin was splitting open as she desperately willed it to come like she'd done so many times before.

Willing something, *anything*, to come out at her from the void. A shard, a glimmer, a whisper of that time.

Anything.

But there was *nothing.* The space under her hand felt empty. There was no vague echo of the life that had once grown there, that she'd apparently been excited about. Not one fragile gossamer thread to which she could cling.

So she did exactly as her father had predicted and cried herself to sleep.

IT TOOK A while for Arabella to lose her head of steam. Logan had tried to ring her but she'd ignored his calls. He took to texting, then, begging to know that she was okay. She'd replied to let him know she was fine, but she needed some time.

He'd thanked her and agreed to give her as long as she needed. It hadn't stopped him from texting but they weren't ones that required a response. Normally, just pictures of Flash or a building in the city that he liked or some titbit from the news or a picture of his lunch or something silly that had happened at work.

Informative and funny and friendly. Absolutely no pressure. Despite her animosity, Arabella had grown quite fond of them and looked forward to her phone vibrating several times a day. Looked forward to the inevitable laugh his texts provided.

A bright patch amidst the dullness of court and the confusion of her life.

She hadn't cried since that night. She hadn't regressed or fallen apart as her father had feared. But she *had* turned everything over and over in her head until she was dizzy with it. In a strangely detached, logical way she had come to understand why her parents had chosen their course of action.

But it had taken a while to *accept*. For the anger to dissipate.

Her amnesia had been piling up layers of rage for four years now. Anger over what it had robbed her of had built incrementally and she'd needed time between each hit to assimilate it. To deal with it.

She usually got there in the end and this was no different.

Rationally, she knew her parents had done what they thought best at the time. She knew from her kind of work that *most* people did the best they could with what they had. Her parents hadn't kept her lost baby from her to hurt her, but to protect her.

No matter how wrong or misplaced that was.

So she'd reached out to them and they were talking again even if it was a little stilted and strained.

Arabella didn't feel similarly charitable towards Logan. There was no logic or detachment where he was concerned. It was *all* seething, roiling emotion. She loved him so much it hurt, which only increased her sense of betrayal. At least her parents had done what they'd done for *her*. Logan had done what he'd done for *them*.

Was it too much to expect the man she loved to be on her side?

She might be looking forward to his texts but she was a long way from forgiving him. From wanting to see him.

But then she woke one Saturday morning, two weeks after she'd found that picture, with such a crushing sense of loss she couldn't even get out of bed. It sat on her chest like an elephant and she couldn't drag herself out from under it.

It was so different from the bizarre disconnection that had haunted her past couple of weeks. Suddenly she knew what she wanted and it was Logan. Or rather the information that only he knew. Sure, she wanted to cry and rage at him and pummel her fists against his chest. She wanted to hurt him, transfer the pain she was feeling to him. But more than anything, she wanted to know about her baby.

Their baby.

A sudden knock on her door startled her. Even before she peered through the peep hole, she knew it was Logan. It was as if her emotional turbulence had conjured him up. Or summonsed him, anyway. She was in her PJ's – one of his T-shirts she'd acquired that fell to mid-thigh and her underwear – but her pulse leapt and her heart leapt and he was outside her door so big and real and she'd *missed* him.

She was still *mad as hell* at him but her gut twisted in such a visceral way that she flung the door open without a moment's hesitation.

"Bella," he said and it scraped along all her nerve endings.

He was so gorgeously male in his soft faded jeans and T-shirt – so *Logan* – she had to hold tight to the door handle to stop herself from bursting into tears.

"I'm sorry, I know you wanted me to stay away but… I just had to see you." His gaze raked her face and her body like he was doing an inventory, checking everything was still were he left it. That she was okay. "I've been so worried about you." He pushed a hand into his hair. "Are you all right?"

Arabella shook her head slowly as one by one the features of her face gave into the emotion that had been threatening since she woke with that elephant on her chest. Her chin dimpled as she sucked air in and out of her lungs trying to prevent the inevitable breakdown. But it was too late, her bottom lip was wobbling and her whole face was collapsing.

It *felt* grotesque – God knew what it looked like.

He took a step towards her, over the threshold of the apartment. "Oh, God, Bella… don't. Please don't."

He held his arms out to her but she took a step back, shaking her head. "I'm st-st-still r-really… p-p-pissed at you." She choked the words out in what must have been a largely unintelligible mess.

"I know," he said, reaching for her, ignoring her feeble head shaking and attempts to ward him off, as he hauled her into his arms. "I know."

Arabella didn't resist any longer. It felt so good. *He* felt so good. Big and solid, shouldering her sobs, absorbing her grief.

"It's okay," he murmured into her hair. "I've got you."

And it was exactly what it felt like. Like he had her. He smelled like he'd just got out of the shower and his arms banded around her like he never wanted to let her go and his heart thumped sure and steady beneath her ear. It felt like she was home. Like she was safe. Like she could tell him anything. Lean on him for anything.

She had no memory of what had happened all those years ago – *none whatsoever* – but it felt really freaking real this morning. The grief over a child she never knew, *didn't even have a memory of*, was suddenly profound and shocking.

And he was the only other person who could truly understand that. In his arms, she knew he understood how she was feeling even when she didn't understand it herself.

He held her until her sobs eased and her tears dried up. Until they were just standing in the middle of her apartment, holding each other.

"Are you okay now?" he asked, when he finally pulled away a little, his eyes locking on hers.

Arabella shook her head. It didn't feel like she'd ever be okay again. "I want to know more. About the baby. About Faith."

He nodded slowly, his Adam's apple bobbing in his throat. "Would you like to see where we buried her?"

Arabella's breath caught in her throat as a warm rush of tears threatened again. *Surely there were no tears left?*

She hadn't thought about a grave. A special place where they'd laid her to rest. She'd barely come to terms with having had a baby let alone that baby's stillbirth.

The fact there was somewhere filled Arabella with immense relief.

"Yes," she whispered. "Very much."

Chapter Fifteen

ARABELLA LISTENED INTENTLY as Logan talked about the pregnancy on the way to the grave. About how they'd been irresponsible and careless. How they'd been caught out a couple of times without condoms but risked it anyway. How they'd been shocked at the unexpected news despite the risks they'd taken. But then happy and excited even through a couple of months of heinous morning sickness.

He told her about her father's visit. About how he'd counselled Arabella to have a termination, to come home, but she'd told her father to go back to Melbourne and get used to the idea of being a grandfather.

She smiled at that.

He told her about the day he came home from work to find her worried that she hadn't felt the baby move since the night before. How they'd gone to the hospital and they'd done an ultrasound and there was no heartbeat. How they'd induced her the next day.

He didn't have to say how devastated they were. She could hear it vibrating in his voice; see it in the clench of his knuckles around the steering wheel.

The sun was warm on Arabella's shoulders as Logan walked her through to their daughter's final resting place. The memorial gardens were surrounded by native trees, the low twitter of birds and drone of insects added to the peaceful ambience.

"Do you come here often?"

"Every now and then. I bring flowers and keep everything neat. Duncan looked after it for me when I was away."

It hadn't occurred to Arabella that others knew about the baby. Just her and Logan and her parents. But, of course, they would have. His family. *Her* brother and sister. Maybe even some of her work colleagues. Who knew how many others?

None of whom had said anything.

He stopped at a plot, edged with a low decorative hedge. Tiny purple flowers pushed through the foliage and it was neatly trimmed. Arabella stared down at the small, low granite gravestone which sat in the middle flanked on either side by two sleeping angels carved from stone. They'd aged and weathered during their vigil. The inscription was simple.

Faith Tucker Knight. Born sleeping.

The words were like a sledgehammer to Arabella's heart and she leaned against Logan. His arm slipped around her shoulders as he tucked her into his side.

Born sleeping.

"She didn't even take *one* breath?" He'd already told her

that their daughter hadn't but to see it in writing…

To see the tiny, little stone and the angels… To know the baby girl in the ground had once lived inside her.

He squeezed her arm. "No."

She pulled away from him and sank to her knees. The lawn prickled her skin and her hip twinged as she reached out and traced the letters on the headstone with an index finger.

Faith Tucker Knight.

"Why Faith?"

It was such an old-fashioned name and no one in her family – as far as she could *remember* – was called Faith.

He sank down beside her, his soft jeans pulling taut over his thighs. "Because we had to have faith that her death had happened for a reason. That she'd come into our lives for a reason. That it wasn't all for nothing."

And yet, it seemed, to Arabella, that it *had* all been for nothing. Especially now when it was only Logan who remembered.

Guilt swamped her chest like a tsunami. "Was it me? Did I do something?" She turned slightly to face him. "Did I drink alcohol? Did I… take drugs? Did I…" She searched around for another reason. "Stand too close to a petrol pump?"

"No." His hands slid onto her upper arms, holding tight. Tears shone in his eyes. "No. *Nothing.* You did everything right and she was *perfect*, she was absolutely perfect."

The pain in his gaze was killing her. Up this close, she could see his anguish, see the march of memories playing across his mind's eye as he relived it all over again. Memories he carried alone now. The weight obviously heavy on his shoulders as his gaze desperately searched hers.

She knew that look. He was willing her to remember. Willing some spark, a glimmer of something that told him he wasn't alone in his misery. Maybe he'd thought bringing her here would be just the emotional jolt she needed. A catalyst that finally opened the vault in her head.

His hands squeezed her upper arms harder as if he was trying to physically transfer his memories. Wanting her to share his burden. *Needing* her to.

"I don't remember," she whispered, her heart thudding painfully in her chest. "I'm sorry but I don't remember. I've been racking my brain, trying to but… it's just a blank."

Her voice cracked and it broke the spell that seemed to have descended upon Logan.

"I'm sorry." He relaxed his hands and pulled her into a hug then, hard and long and they clung to each other for what seemed an age, the dull ache in her hip ignored.

He pulled back eventually, his eyes no longer shiny, but his mouth set in a grim line. "The doctors don't know why it happened," he said, picking up where he'd left off. "It just… does sometimes, that's all."

Logically, Arabella knew that but what if it *had* been something she'd done? "Could they have performed an autopsy?"

Thinking clinically, thinking like a lawyer, helped keep the guilt at bay.

"Yes." He nodded. "But… we couldn't bear the thought of her… being cut open."

Arabella's gut clenched tight and a hot rush of tears brimmed in her eyes. Guilt was replaced by a swift jab of reality. She hadn't thought about what an autopsy meant and she suddenly couldn't bear the thought of it either. The threatening tears spilled down her cheeks.

He stroked them away with his thumb. "We're a fine pair, aren't we?" he murmured, his smile achingly sad as he tried to lighten the mood.

She returned it with a lopsided one of her own. "How can I be so sad about a baby I don't even remember?"

"Because you're human. You *feel* things. You don't have to have a personal connection with death or tragedy to be sad or sorry it happened." He smiled and it reached his eyes this time. "It's called empathy."

Arabella nodded. "But…" And this was the real question. The one she'd seen in each of their gazes more than once. The one she still didn't know the answer to. "How can I *not* remember? A baby. *Our* baby. Of all things?"

He shrugged. "I don't know."

There wasn't any judgment in his statement, but just like the guilt, Arabella felt it anyway.

"I have a few more photos at home if you'd like to see

them."

Part of her shied from the brutal honesty of the photograph she'd already seen. Not sure if she was strong enough to look at others. But there was a much bigger part of her that *yearned* to see them. And it would not be denied.

"Thank you," she said and slipped her hand into his.

FLASH WAS ECSTATIC to see her, practically wriggling himself into a knot. Arabella laughed as she cuddled his shimmying body, some of the dread and tension that had been building on their way to Logan's eased.

"Hey, Bella," Duncan said from the kitchen, looking uneasily from Arabella to his brother back to Arabella again. "Good to see you around here again."

"I'm just coming to see some photos."

"Oh… right." He glanced at Logan again with concerned eyes. "That's cool."

Damn right it was *cool.* Her resentment against Logan stirred again and Duncan by association. "You knew about the baby."

He swallowed. "Yes."

"You knew he hadn't said anything to me about her."

Another quick glance at Logan. "Yes. For what it's worth I did tell him he was dumber than a box of rocks for agreeing to your father's request, even dumber than when he let you go in the first place."

Logan shifted uncomfortably but Arabella was touched by Duncan's words and gave a watery smile despite how mad she was at the situation. She appreciated Duncan for trying to lighten the mood.

"Yeah, well... Like I said, I'm just here to look at some photos."

"They're on my computer," Logan said, shooting his brother a brief look before his hand hovered in the small of her back and he herded her towards his bedroom.

He offered her the computer chair and she sat, her heart beating loud in anticipation as he powered up the PC and navigated around the screen. Arabella was rooted to the spot, torn between wanting to run far away and wanting to stay, to see more of her baby.

"This is them," he said quietly as he clicked on a folder titled August.

There were only four in total, including the one she'd already seen. Two with her holding the baby – holding *Faith* – two with Logan holding her. Neither of them was looking at the camera, they only had eyes for their daughter, locked inside a heinous tunnel of grief.

Arabella's hand lifted to the screen and she traced the tiny hand, translucent in its prematurity. Her eyes were closed and she did just look... asleep. "Who took them?"

"The midwife did."

"I can't believe we had the wherewithal to request pictures," she murmured. They looked utterly sucker-punched.

"We didn't. She took them anyway. On Duncan's phone. He was outside the entire time, refusing to leave. She knew we'd want them at some stage, that we'd appreciate them. I don't think this was her first stillbirth."

A thickening in Arabella's throat threatened to cut off her air supply. Both at Duncan posting vigil at the hospital and the forethought of a nurse – a total stranger – who'd known what they were going to need even when they hadn't because her job was to care for everyone, whether their babies lived or not.

God. Arabella's eyes watered. What a terrible thing to ask of another human being.

"Did we?" She half turned in the chair. He was standing behind her, his eyes glued to the screen, his hands shoved in his pockets. "Appreciate it?"

He nodded. "We looked at them often."

"Do you still look at them?"

"I did a lot after you–" He took a deep breath. "When you went back to Melbourne. But only occasionally these last few years."

Arabella turned back, staring at the screen again. She clicked from photo to photo, enlarging each one so she could see the details. She was vaguely aware that Logan had moved away but it was another twenty minutes before she'd looked her fill and could drag her attention back to the here and now and not the cloying misery of a hospital room nine years ago.

She turned to find him sitting on the end of his bed, watching and waiting patiently, Flash stretched out on his feet. His face was still a mask, his chin dimple nowhere in sight.

"Thank you," she said, pushing to her feet with what felt like great effort. Her whole body felt heavy, weighted down by grief.

"Of course." He dismissed it as if it was no big deal.

She shook her head. She didn't want him to dismiss it as nothing. He'd taken her to their daughter's grave, spoken about her, told Arabella all the things she should already know.

It must have been hell on him.

"No, I mean it. I know this hasn't been easy on you today. That *none* of this has been easy on you. I think maybe it would have been better if we'd never met up again."

Maybe her father was right? What good had it done for her to know what she knew now? To be weighed down by secondhand grief?

"No." He crossed the short distance between them. "No, Bella." His grey eyes were shining as his hands slid onto her upper arms and she wondered if he was fighting back tears. "I will always be grateful for whatever fates brought us back together again."

"Really?" She wasn't so sure, an unbearable sadness sinking into her bones. "Even the way it is now? The way it… ended up?"

These last few months had been some of the happiest of her life but all she could feel now was the heavy ache in her heart.

Despair prowled in his gaze as he searched hers for long wrenching moments. “I know you’re still mad at me and you have every right to be but it doesn’t have to end, Bella. Couldn’t we start again? Wipe the slate clean?”

His request was like a dagger to her soul. She wanted nothing more than to be with him but she wasn’t sure after today that Logan could ever come to terms with her memory loss and that would be the death of them.

She couldn’t be in a relationship with him, knowing who she was now would never be enough for him. Knowing he would always be looking for the old Bella.

“I’m not mad at you. Not anymore.” How could she be after today? “I know my father put you between a rock and a hard place and you were just trying to do the right thing.”

He didn’t say anything, just watched her with solemn eyes, waiting.

“But…” She shook his hands off her arms and they slid away. “I don’t think we can start again, either.”

Even the words wounded her. Her heart was breaking wide open but she knew with absolute certainty she was right.

“We can,” he insisted. “If we love each other enough, we can do whatever we want.”

Arabella swallowed the lump in her throat. *If only that*

were so. "I do love you, Logan. I do. But… I'm not the woman I was. And I don't think this new me is going to be enough for you."

His mouth tightened to a grim line. "Why don't you let me be the judge of that?"

"Logan." Her voice cracked. "I'm *never* going to remember what we had. I'm *never* going to remember carrying your baby. I'm *never* going to remember what that felt like. But you look at me like that…"

She shook her head and the lump doubled in her throat threatening to choke her. "And I feel that you're reliving our baby's death over and over again and it kills me because I can't remember and I know you want me to. You keep looking at me like if I just applied myself a little better or a little longer, it'll all come back."

"That's not true," he denied.

But Arabella could hear the uncertainty in his voice. "I can't live under that kind of pressure, Logan. Like I'm somehow defective, like it's my fault, like I'm not trying hard enough. You want to love me then you have to love me and accept me for who I am now. Not who I was nine years ago. I'm not that person. She's gone, Logan. And she's never coming back."

He looked helpless for a moment, like he wanted to deny everything but he couldn't. "Bella."

His voice was a rough whisper, which clawed at her heart. If one word could contain all his grief and loss and longing it was that. The slow tear that slid from his eye, hammered straight into the middle of her chest.

She blinked back her own grief. If she cracked, even a little, she'd spend the rest of her life in the shadow of a ghost. "I have to go."

She backed away from him and he let her, watching her with misery weighing his shoulders down. She turned and headed for his door.

"Will you go back to Melbourne?"

His question pulled her up just as she stood in the doorway. "I don't know…" she said, not turning to address him. She hadn't thought that far. Her plans had been to stay on here but she couldn't do that now. Going home didn't appeal either.

Maybe she'd head to Fiji or Bali for a while. Somewhere she could be herself with absolutely no expectations from anyone.

Get a suntan while she was at it.

"The case has another two weeks to run so… I'll make up my mind then."

"Can I see you before you go?"

Arabella shook her head. Why? What purpose would it serve other than shredding their hearts just a little bit more? "I don't think that's a good idea. I think we need a clean break."

Bracing her shoulders, she walked out of his room. But there was still Duncan to contend with. Duncan who had refused to leave the hospital.

"Bella?" His expression was neutral but she could see the worry in his eyes. Duncan was fond of her, but she had no doubt he was team Logan all the way.

She took a deep, shaky breath so her voice wouldn't wobble. "Take care of him, will you?"

He looked like he was going to say something then thought better of it and just nodded.

It made it easier to leave. A little.

Chapter Sixteen

When the call came for the factory fire Logan was spoiling for a fight. A huge, roaring inferno licking heat and flames and smoke was just the focus his rage needed. He'd heard today that the investigation into his grandfather would likely drag on for most of the year and it had been two weeks exactly since Bella had walked out of his life.

His degree of pissed-off had reached epic proportions.

"Hot diggity dog," Duncan said, letting rip a low appreciative whistle. "That's a monster."

"Fucking A," Logan agreed, watching the flames and thick black smoke spew into the air, turning the blue sky above into a churning, black cauldron. Just like his mood. "Let me at it."

The fire was everything Logan needed right now. Big and raging and hungry. He couldn't do a damn thing about his private life but he could beat this motherfucker into submission and that was exactly what he intended to do. He leapt out of the truck before it had even come to a complete stop.

The scene was the usual controlled chaos of a huge fire. A dozen engines as well as police and ambulance dotting the area. The building was an old, abandoned warehouse in the docks area, its brick exterior holding its own – so far – even if the windows and roof had not.

It was also a well-known squat. Logan hoped like hell no one was inside because the building was well alight and too dangerous for anyone to go in on a rescue mission. A hot westerly wind slapped against his cheek. That was going to be a real problem for the other buildings in the vicinity if they came under ember attack from the burning warehouse.

A surge of adrenaline flooded Logan's system as they took their orders from the on scene commander and then it was all hands on deck. It felt good to be able to do something. He'd been feeling so damn hamstrung for the last two weeks trying to respect Bella's wishes about a clean break but finally he was *doing* something. *Taking control* of something. Immersing himself in something that required *all* of his concentration, *all* of his focus.

Stationed on a hose, he directed all his energies towards the hungry flames and got lost in the process of fighting a fire.

It was him against the flames and he revelled in it.

Logan was good at his job. Exceptionally good. He had the Knight gift for it. There was no fear of the fire that would turn most mortals to jelly because flames licked in his blood. To him it was a battle – good against evil.

And he was the good guy.

His whole world narrowed down to the stream of water and the leap of orange, fork-tongued flames. He was conscious only of his brother firefighters around him going about their business as if they were all participating in some elaborate choreographed ballet. Everyone was dancing their own well-rehearsed parts but always with an eye on each other, anticipating moves and adjusting accordingly. Guys like Duncan and Ruth and the others he shared shifts, beers, and trivia with, all working towards the same goal.

There was no time to think about his life. About how he was going to keep putting one foot in front of the other into the future. About Bella leaving soon. *Too soon.* About what he could say or do to change her mind.

About whether he *should*.

Or whether he should just accept that he and Bella were never destined to be together. Hell, twice fate had brought them together and twice it had torn them apart. Surely there was a message there somewhere?

But there was no room for that now. There was just him and the fire.

It was hot, hard work. The fire was ferocious and hungry and it took a dozen trucks and their crews six hours to bring it under control and another two to extinguish it altogether.

The day was turning to night when Logan came out of his trance. Back to the real world. To the grotesque scene in front of him – the garish strobe of emergency vehicle lights flashing across the blackened shell of the smoking building.

His muscles bitched and ached, he had a raging thirst, smoke clung to his clothes and soot clogged his nostrils. He didn't have to look at himself to know his face would be thick with grime. That it would be in his ears and his nose and in dried rivulets down his chest and back from the sweat that had poured off him all day.

But they'd won.

Ruth smiled at him and put her hand up for a high five. "Who ya gonna call?" she said.

Logan smiled back, his arms almost too damn weary to clap his hand against hers. *Almost.* "Another one bites the dust."

"Kicked its ass," she agreed with a wide grin as Logan tipped his head back and downed a litre of water without pausing for a breath.

It wasn't over though. There were hot spots to check and a fatality search to be conducted and Logan wanted to be part of it. Not because he wanted to find anyone's charred remains but because he wanted to make sure the sonofabitch was actually out.

He went in with Duncan and Ruth half an hour later. It was getting towards the end of their shift and no one would have thought twice about them packing up and heading home. But they'd hydrated and eaten and nothing was going to stop them from finishing what they came here to do.

They were given an area to search on the fourth floor and

their mood was chipper as they went into the smouldering remains. Considering the potential hazards they were decidedly upbeat. But they wore their breathing apparatus and were trained professionals who had confidence in themselves and each other.

The internal structure of the building had been a mix of brick and concrete and wood. The warehouse had undergone several different internal fit-outs over the years most of which were evident from the charred rubble left behind by the fire. They had to be careful where they walked although Logan doubted any timber was left after the fire.

"A bath," Ruth said, as they methodically picked their way through the fourth floor segment. Their masks were designed to amplify their voices. "First thing I'm going to do when I get home is soak in a bath for an hour."

"Wash your mouth out Gilligan," Duncan said in faux horror. "First thing is always a beer."

"Oh, I'm going to be drinking a beer as well," she said. "It's called multitasking. But you wouldn't know about that because of the whole penis thing."

"A wet, naked, beer drinking woman." Duncan didn't appear to be insulted at all by Ruth's slight against the male of the species. "Why aren't we together again, Gilligan?"

"Because you're a pervert who wouldn't know monogamy if it bit you on the ass."

"This is true."

"Plus, you couldn't handle a strong, black woman."

"You might be surprised what I can handle, Gilligan."

Ruth snorted. "You can't even handle your coffee black. That sissy frothy shit you drink is an insult to coffee. I'm surprised your penis doesn't retract inside your body every time you take a sip."

"You're awfully interested in my dick, Gilligan."

Logan tuned them out. He was used to Duncan and Ruth bickering like an old married couple and all he could think about was what he wanted to do after *he* left here.

He wanted to see Bella. *Needed* to see her. Fate be damned. If they were truly not meant to be together, she wouldn't have appeared back in his life again. *That* was his sign from the universe. The rest didn't matter.

As soon as he was done here, he was heading home, cleaning up then going straight to her place and he didn't give a good goddamn about a clean break. This was love.

Love was *messy*.

Bella had been right. He *had* been hoping deep down inside that the revelation of the baby would be the key to unlocking her amnesia. That somehow the trauma of the baby's loss had taken advantage of her head injury, like some kind of parasite. That it had used the head trauma to hide the baby trauma, hijacked her amnesia and given Bella a psychological way out of the grief and memories.

Even if it had meant taking everything else with it.

And with everything revealed, with that memory dragged out into the light and shown to her, he'd hoped all the memories would come flooding back.

Those nine missing years in all their grief and glory.

He hadn't even dared think it out loud but it was true.

The brain *did* work in mysterious ways, right? And there were many things medical science just couldn't explain.

But it hadn't happened that way. Sure, there'd been grief when she'd found out about Faith. But not *recognition*. Not *memory*. Not when she'd looked at the photos or listened to him talk about the pregnancy or stood by their daughter's grave.

She'd felt the loss as a normal human reaction, not as Faith's *mother*.

And he had to accept that the woman he'd shared *that* experience with nine years ago was lost. Probably forever.

He could do that.

Because the woman he'd fallen in love with was still here. It was still Bella. Things had changed between them, sure. He wasn't some young guy high on sex and hormones and she wasn't high on freedom and rebellion anymore. They were both older and wiser. Matured. Tempered.

Better.

And Bella… Bella was braver and stronger and fiercer then she'd ever been and he loved her more than he'd ever done. More than he ever knew was possible.

So… he was going to go and get her back. He'd beg if he had to, he wasn't too proud for that. Hell, he'd move to Melbourne if he had to.

Because she was the fire that lit his soul.

"I'm just sayin'," Duncan said as Logan tuned back in, "I thought maybe you secretly batted for the other side but clearly you have a serious fixation with my penis."

Logan laughed. Duncan was still talking about his favourite subject – his cock.

Ruth laughed hysterically. "If anything was going to make me bat for the other side it'd be your penis."

"Jesus, you two," Logan said. "You should really do it already and get it over with."

"You heard the man, Gilligan," Duncan said, slapping his brother on the back.

"Not if you were the last man on earth."

Logan turned around to face them. "Do you think we can have less of the sexually frustrated banter and a little more hustle? I have some major grovelling to do with the woman I love and I'd like to get to it as soon as possible."

"Yeah?" Duncan's soot-smudged face beamed at Logan though the clear panel of his mask and Logan couldn't help but smile back.

Before he could answer, a large crack rent the air and they all looked up as a chunk of ceiling that hadn't fallen already tore loose and plummeted down.

"Shit," Logan said, diving quickly out of its way as it came at him.

He hit the ground shoulder first, a starburst of pain erupting across the joint as the chunk thunked to the ground landing a foot from his right leg.

"*Logan!*" Duncan voice seemed to come from a very long way away as Logan's vision greyed from the searing agony in his shoulder. "Bloody hell, are you alright?"

His brother's concerned, sooty face, floated over top of him and was the last thing Logan saw as his vision went completely black.

~

ARABELLA HAD BEEN packing when she got the call. If it'd been Logan she would have ignored it but it had been Duncan and a sudden spike of dread had her snatching the phone up without a second thought.

Looking at Logan now through a gap in the curtains she was pleased he had. He was lying semi-reclined and passed out on a hospital gurney, his face and clothes streaked with soot and reeking of smoke.

They'd obviously taken to his shirt with some scissors. Half of it still clung to his torso but the right side had been hacked away to get to the injured joint. A sturdy-looking sling with thick Velcro straps was now in place securing his arm close to his body, leaving his shoulder and half his soot-streaked upper chest bare.

He seemed so pale and still and her heart skipped a beat as she waited – *and waited* – for him to take a breath so she could see he was still alive. It seemed to take an age for his chest to expand and she released a ragged breath when it finally complied with her desperate mental urgings.

"It's okay," Duncan said softly from behind her. "You can go closer. It's only a dislocated shoulder."

But what if it had been worse?

The fear that had gripped her during her ride to the hospital intensified.

What if it had been worse?

And the last thing he remembered of her was her telling him that a clean break was best?

Not that she loved him. That she would always love him.

She approached slowly, worry and fear and guilt weighing each footstep down. Duncan had told her they'd given him some drugs to put the shoulder back in and he was sleeping it off. But what if it was worse than that? What if he'd lapsed into unconsciousness? What if he'd banged his head as well and his brain was silently bleeding inside the confines of his rigid skull?

Had he had a CT? An MRI? What about his ribs? Had they done a chest x-ray?

God, she hated hospitals. Nothing but bad memories in every set of white sheets and blue curtains. The clinical, antiseptic smell something from her nightmares.

She stood by his gurney, looking down at him, feeling about as helpless as she always had in hospital. The cleft in his chin was ironed out in his slumber and she suppressed the urge to touch it, to reassure herself it was still there. She wasn't game to wake him or touch him. Or make any kind of movement around him.

But her heart was turning over in her chest and expanding like crazy. She'd missed him so much. He looked pale and exhausted and she loved him.

The last of her anger over him not telling her about Faith disappeared. There were clearly bigger things to worry about.

Her gaze was drawn to the white sheets and the mess he was making of them. It looked like someone had *tried* to clean his face but not very well and there were smudges of soot from his uniform dirtying the sheets wherever his body came into contact. His big, black boots were also filthy with it but at least they were hanging over the end and safe from besmirching the pristine fabric.

For a moment she felt sorry for him. Nurses were never pleased with dirty sheets.

One bustled in then and proved Arabella completely wrong as she picked up his chart then cast *more* than a professional eye over Logan's big, slumbering body. Arabella supposed a big hunk of sooty, dirty fireman could be forgiven anything.

Even dirty sheets.

The nurse bustled out again leaving Arabella alone with Logan for a second or two before she sensed Duncan approaching.

He pulled up on the opposite side of the gurney. "You okay?" he asked.

Duncan blinked at her from out of eyes ringed with soot

giving him an almost comical raccoon appearance. She nodded because she didn't trust her voice.

"You can wake him you know. He won't mind."

"Oh, no." She shook her head. "Let him sleep, he looks done in."

But Duncan apparently didn't feel any such compunction. "Hey, Sleeping Beauty," he said in a low, commanding voice so similar to his brother's. "Wake up, you have a visitor."

Arabella held her breath as Logan's eyes fluttered open and took a second to focus and another second or two to process what he was seeing. "Bella?" He tried to sit up but froze and sucked in a quick breath as his shoulder obviously protested.

"Don't move," she said hastily, placing a hand on his uninjured shoulder.

"What are you doing here?"

Arabella frowned, confused for a moment at the question and his apparent annoyance. He didn't want her here?

"I called her," Duncan said.

Logan rolled his head to the other side to glare at his brother. "Why?"

"You'd asked for her a couple of times."

"I was *high,*" he said, exasperated.

"That's usually when we say the things we want the most," Duncan said drily obviously not concerned by his brother's irritability.

"Look at her man, now she's all worried. And she needn't because I'm fine."

"I wish you two would stop talking about me like I'm not here."

He rolled his head back to face her. "I'm fine, really," he continued. "It's just a dislocated shoulder. It doesn't even really hurt anymore–"

"Except if you try to sit up," Duncan interrupted.

Logan ignored him, his gaze boring into hers. "It just needs a sling for a couple of weeks, that's all."

"He'll be off work for at least four," Duncan added.

"God, Bella. Please stop looking at me like that, I'm fine really."

She didn't know how she was looking, only how she was feeling. Just a dislocated shoulder. *This time.* "What if it had been worse?" The words slipped out before she could stop them. Her worst fear out there.

"It wasn't."

The curtain snapped open wider to reveal the nurse from earlier and another woman who appeared to be somewhere in her fifties wearing civvies instead of scrubs, a stethoscope slung around her neck.

"Good to see you're awake." She didn't introduce herself so Arabella assumed she was the doctor who'd performed the relocation.

"Yes."

"How's your pain?"

"Shit loads better than it was."

A small smile lifted the corner of her mouth. "On a scale of one to ten?"

"One."

Her eyebrow kicked up in a purely disbelieving motion and Logan sighed. "Three."

"Atta boy." She patted him on the leg. "Well you can go home. But the sling stays on for two weeks. No driving in that time. No heavy lifting or fighting fires for four weeks. Follow up appointment in a month. I've written you a script for some painkillers."

He shot the doctor a that-won't-be-necessary look. Arabella opened her mouth to protest but the doctor was way ahead of her. "We don't give out badges for bravery here, Mr. Knight. If you're in pain you won't do your physio. If you don't do your physio your shoulder won't get better. If your shoulder doesn't get better, I won't clear you for work. Do you see where I'm going with this?"

"Hard ball, huh?"

"That's my middle name. Now…" she said, "I'm assuming that any of the dozen sooty firefighters chatting up my nurses outside will be able to transport you home?"

Duncan put up his hand. "I'll drive him."

"No." A possessive roar flared through Arabella's veins.

Abso-*freaking*-lutely not.

No one but her was taking him home. "*I* will."

Chapter Seventeen

LOGAN COULDN'T REMEMBER hearing two more beautiful words in his life. Even if she had volunteered so she could ream him a new one, he was on board with that. Because Bella had come to him. He could have killed Duncan for worrying her but… *she had come.* And he was clinging to that.

Not that she got the chance to yell at him once he was safely ensconced in the car half an hour later because he fell asleep almost instantly. From fatigue, exhaustion, the residual effects of heavy duty narcotics and the kind of peace of mind he hadn't had in two weeks.

Because she'd come.

It felt like he'd been asleep for a day when his door opened and he prised his eyelids open. "We're here," she said, crouched down beside him.

He smiled at her. She was a sight for sore eyes. And a sore body. "Your hire car is going to reek of smoke," he murmured, conscious his words sounded slightly slurred.

"I'll get it detailed," she dismissed, standing briskly then hovering as he eased out of the vehicle.

When they reached the lifts she insisted on rolling the door up and pulling the cage open. "The doctor said no heavy lifting."

He watched her grimace with the effort of manoeuvring the heavy steel and stepped in to help, the last thing they needed was her dislocating her hip. She put a hand on his chest to stop him.

"There's nothing wrong with my left arm," he grumbled.

"Humour me. You're going to be doing that a lot tonight."

Logan was pretty sure she didn't mean that as some kind of sexy come on but, whether it was the drugs or the fact that she'd come to the hospital, his body was totally going there.

Things stirred. Things that clearly weren't as fatigued or as drug affected as the rest of him.

"Oh, yeah?" he murmured as he stepped into the lift and she shut the cage behind them. "What do you plan on doing to me?"

"I'm putting you in the bath. Then I'm putting you to bed."

Well... fuck. *That* didn't really help with the stirring problem no matter how businesslike she'd said it. He wanted bath and bed too but mostly he wanted her.

"Yes, ma'am."

She didn't respond. In fact she didn't seem in any kind of mood to use her words and Logan didn't push. They were clearly going to have to talk but just being with her was enough for now. Frankly, he was too damn exhausted to string a sentence together.

Flash was ecstatic to see Bella and she paused to give him some love as Logan continued into the bedroom. He wanted out of his smoky clothes. He'd just toed off his boots when Bella joined him, Flash at her heels. Their gazes locked for a moment before she headed for his en suite and he heard the sound of water hitting porcelain.

"Stay, Flash," he said then crossed to the bathroom and stood in the doorway, checking out the curve of her ass as she bent slightly at the hips to check the temperature in his bathtub. She was wearing some kind of loose track pants which sat low on her hips.

"Hot," he said.

She looked over her shoulder at him, clocking his interest in her butt.

"The bath." He smiled. "Nice and hot."

He needed it to ease into all his muscles and soothe their aches. She turned back and twisted the hot tap a little more until a satisfying puff of steam rose from the rapidly filling bath.

Logan used his good hand to undo the buttons of his shirt – what was left of it. He vaguely remembered hearing the shearing noise of scissors but he'd been in too much pain to pay it any heed. The only thing he remembered with any kind of clarity was the moment the drugs had finally hit. The relief had been euphoric.

No wonder people became drug addicts.

He was grappling with the buttons beneath the cumbersome sling when she crossed to him and placed her hand over his. "Let me."

He swallowed. "I can undress myself."

"I know. But you're almost out on your feet and you only have one arm so…"

She made short work of the buttons, easing the shirt off his good shoulder and gently peeling away the tattered remains from the rest of his body.

She tossed it aside before her hand strayed to his trousers. "You want me to stop?" Her gaze locked with his, her fingers cool against his belly as they fiddled with the top button of his fly.

Logan's blood pounded thick and heavy through his veins. He *should* say yes. He could undress himself albeit a little awkwardly.

"No."

His eyes fluttered closed as her fingernails scraped over his rapidly hardening cock. There was nothing lingering or caressing about her movement, it was brisk and methodical and he doubted she was aware of the effect she was having on him as she undid the five buttons.

Logan opened his eyes to find her watching him. She smelled good. So good. Although compared to his sweaty, smoky self that wouldn't be hard. Her hands shifted to his hips, fingers hooking under his waistband but he stopped her with a rough noise at the back of his throat. He wanted to warn her at least about his arousal.

"I'm afraid there's a little... excitement going on down there."

Both eyebrows winged upwards. "Oh..."

She seemed genuinely surprised and he dredged up a smile. "What did you think would happen when you talked about bathing me and putting me to bed then started undressing me?"

Her throat bobbed and he almost groaned out loud. "But... you're exhausted."

"Yes. Exhausted. Not *dead*." He gestured vaguely to his pants.

She glanced down at the flaps of his open fly then back at him again. "Well that's... inconvenient."

Logan gave her a ghost of a smile. "You have no idea."

For long moments she didn't say anything then she nodded as if she'd made up her mind. "Come on," she said, "let's get you into the bath."

She stripped his trousers and his underwear down his legs in one smooth movement, crouching in front of him as she eased them off his feet. His aching quads trembled at the sight of her at his feet, her blonde head bent over the job. He gave her extra marks for valiantly ignoring the hard jut of his cock as she tossed his trousers aside then stripped off his socks.

"Bath," she said, standing, still ignoring the elephant in the room.

It felt like a bloody elephant too – big and hard and long. And difficult to unsee.

Logan sighed and reached around to the Velcro joining at his neck to undo the sling but she slid a hand on his arm and said, "Wait until the last moment to take it off."

Her hand slid away as she turned back to the bath. It was one of those trendy oval freestanding tubs just a little out from, and parallel to, the far bathroom wall. The taps jutted off the wall at the midpoint leaving plenty of room to move around at both ends. A flat shelf next to the taps housed his soap and shampoo.

Steam rose from the three-quarter full tub as she turned the water off. "That's *hot*," she said, trailing her fingers over the surface.

"Good."

Logan grimaced as he lifted first one leg then the other into the water. It *was* hot but not unbearably so. Hot enough to work magic on his muscles and hopefully too hot for his annoyingly persistent erection. He lifted his hand again but her fingers beat him to it, light and cool against his neck.

"Hold your arm close."

He did as he was instructed, taking the weight of his limb as she undid the Velcro fasteners and eased the sling away.

"Okay?" she asked, her voice husky.

His shoulder ached slightly more than the rest of him but compared to the pain from earlier it was a walk in the park.

He nodded. "It really isn't hurting that much anymore."

He kept his injured arm close as he grabbed the side of the tub with his good hand and lowered himself slowly into the hot depths, every muscle protesting. He groaned and shut his eyes as he settled his head against the end.

"So good," he muttered as the water enveloped him and cushioned his injured shoulder. He loved that he could stretch out in a bathtub that was big enough to accommodate his size.

Her voice drifted to him he didn't know how many minutes later. "Logan?"

"Mmmm?" He forced heavy eyelids open to look at her.

She handed him the girly, purple loofah thingy she'd left in his shower and he hadn't been able to bring himself to throw out. "Use this."

He took it without protest, shutting his eyes again. He knew he had to get clean, he knew how filthy he must be, he just wanted a minute or two to enjoy the heat and weightlessness of the water. And, hey, at least his erection had deflated.

The next thing he knew there was a hand on his good shoulder, squeezing lightly and he roused again. It felt like an hour but the water was still good and hot.

"Scoot forward."

Logan frowned and looked over his shoulder at bare

thighs. His gaze travelled up her body. Up, up, up. Her legs weren't the only things that were bare. A ceramic jug hid the juncture of her thighs from his view but everything else was on display.

Suddenly he felt very, very awake. "You're joining me?"

"You're done in," she said simply. "Now scoot."

He stared at her for long moments, keeping his gaze trained on her face. If she hadn't been here he'd have had to take care of this himself. But she was.

"I'm filthy." He wasn't sure why he was protesting so much. Except he knew what colour the bath water was after a long day of fighting fires.

"Lucky we have soap then."

Logan took in the determined jut of her chin and gave in to temptation. He bent his knees, braced his injured arm against his chest, grabbed the side of the tub and hauled himself upright to allow her to slip in behind him. The water level crept up as she settled in.

So did his dick.

No part of her was touching him but her nearness was a tangible force behind him. "Tip your head back. I'll wash your hair."

Logan did what he was told. His short hair wasn't exactly hard to manage but he was too damn tired and too damn turned on to protest. The thought of her hands on him was irresistible.

The thought of her taking care of him even more so.

Hot water sluiced over his head and down his neck and back followed quickly by her fingers in his hair, massaging his scalp. He was incapable of thinking of anything else. His brain cells went to mush. So did his body. Everything melting and liquefying.

Mostly everything anyway…

His eyes closed and his skin broke out in goose bumps as she kept up the drugging massage, his nipples contracting with each scrape of her fingernails. When her hands finally left his scalp it was only to continue the slow, torturous massage lower. The soft, scratchy fabric of that girly-assed loofah travelled down his nape and around the front of his neck.

She dragged it across his good shoulder and arm right down to his fingers then squeezed the soap out of it over the top of his bad one before ever so gently whispering it over the injured joint and down that arm. His back came next, the loofah gliding with soapy ease over every contour, all the way down to the top of his buttocks.

"Head back again." Her voice wasn't much higher than a whisper.

Logan obeyed and more warm water was sluiced over him, her hand sifting through his hair as she poured and poured, ridding it and his body of every last soap bubble.

By the time she was done his body was humming and desire thrummed at every pulse point.

And she hadn't done the front yet.

"Lay back," she whispered in his ear, her hand sliding onto his good shoulder, urging him backwards.

He didn't need to be asked twice as he surrendered to the pull and eased his body down into the cradle of hers. His head fitted into the crook of her shoulder and his back was plastered along her front. He could feel the soft squash of her breasts and the hard points of her nipples pebbled against his shoulder blades. He was conscious of her parted legs, bent at the knees, her thighs bracketing his hips. Conscious too that she could see right down his body to the taut, heaviness of his erection.

She didn't say anything, though. Just lay quietly, one hand gently splashing warm water over the exposed area of his chest.

He didn't know what this meant, her being with him here like this. Would she have tended to him so lovingly if she was still planning on going back to Melbourne? Before the accident his plan had been to seek her out tonight and beg her to take him back, to give him a second chance.

But she'd come to him. And he wasn't going to squander this opportunity. There were things he needed to say.

"I'm sorry."

His apology sat in the silence between them for long, agonising moments. Her hand stopped its swishing through the water, her muscles tensed beneath him and for a beat or two he thought she might not say anything.

But then she sighed and her body relaxed slightly. "We

don't have to talk about this now."

"Yes, we do." He couldn't live another night without her by his side. He took a slow, deep breath. "I shouldn't have let your father sway me from what I knew to be right."

Her cheek rubbed against his temple as she shook her head. "It's fine, Logan." Her hand squeezed his good shoulder. "I understand. Really. I meant what I said a couple of weeks ago. I'm not mad about it anymore."

Yes, but then she'd walked way, asked for a clean break. Today she'd come to him and he hoped like hell that boded well. But first, there were more apologies to make.

"There's more," he continued. "You were right. I have been waiting…hoping deep down that something might happen between us that would trigger a memory for you. I was gutted when you told me about it, when you said it'd been four years and there'd been nothing, that most people don't get their memories back. But then you knew Flash's name and I started to hope that this was the place where your amnesia might be resolved."

He still remembered the flare of hope he'd felt that day. Now he didn't care about their past. Only their future.

"Started to hope that our love might be the key. That *I* might be the key. I especially thought that Faith might be some kind of catalyst for your memory." And he'd hurt her in the process. "But that was selfish and unfair of me. I know it put an enormous amount of pressure on you and I really *do* understand that your memory's probably never coming back."

"I'm sorry." Her hand tightened its grip on his shoulder. "You don't know how much I wish that wasn't the case."

He did know. He could hear it in her voice. He knew if he turned around he'd see it stamped all over her face. "Don't go to Melbourne." His heart slammed against his rib cage so hard she must surely be able to feel it. "I love you. I've never stopped loving you. Stay here and let me love you properly this time. Let's start over. Looking forward this time, not back."

ARABELLA'S HEART ALMOST burst with emotion. Looking *forward* with Logan – with the man she *loved* – was exactly what she wanted. She'd wanted it even as she was packing her bags but it took him on a hospital gurney to realise she wanted it regardless of whether he could let go of the past or not.

Because *their* past – their love, their relationship, their baby – was very much part of his *present* life. It would be impossible for him to just wipe it from his memory banks.

As impossible as it was for her to gain it back.

She shifted. Slowly – *gently* – sliding out from under him on his non injured side and rolling onto her stomach to face him, chest to chest, her legs floating free over top of his. All the heavy talk had taken care of his erection but she was conscious of his nudity and of hers.

She'd tried to bath him with complete detachment but she was no nurse. The way his muscles had quivered beneath her touch, the way he'd groaned all soft and ragged had tugged at her deep and low. By the time she'd finished she'd been practically groaning herself.

Not that she'd finished really – his face was a testament to that. It was cleaner than it had been but there was still grime where his earlobes met his jawline and around his nostrils and in the cleft of his chin. It clung stubbornly to the fine lines in his forehead and ringed his eyes like black kohl.

"Looking forward could be easier said than done." She wanted him to know she understood his dilemma too. That she wasn't the only injured party where her amnesia was concerned.

"I'm not going to forget it, forget us, Bella, and, yeah, I guess there'll always be a little part of me that will hope for a miracle." He brushed her damp fringe off her forehead with his good hand. "I'm just not going to let it interfere in our relationship from now on."

"You think you can let go of that girl from the past, huh?"

He gave her a tired smile which was crazy sexy. "God… I was hopelessly infatuated with that girl." He shook his head and she could see the self-deprecation in his gaze. "But *she* wasn't the woman sitting outside the firehouse that day. *You* were. She wasn't the one I fell in love with all over again. I fell in love with *you*."

His good hand slid onto the small of her back and she shivered at the touch, her skin erupting in goose bumps.

"And I want to make a whole lifetime of *new* memories with you. If you'll have me. What do you say?"

Tears threatened as Bella's heart suddenly felt too big for her chest. What did she say?

"Yes," she whispered. "A million times yes."

She shifted, grounding her knees against the bottom of the tub, disturbing the water as she straddled him, sitting back slightly. The cooler air caused her nipples to pebble and the way his gaze dropped and widened as he looked his fill grabbed big handfuls of her gut and squeezed.

She grabbed the tub edges with her hands and leaned in to kiss him, quick and hard. She was careful not to jostle him but she needed it more than oxygen. His deep groan slid straight between her legs where his erection was making itself known again.

She was breathing erratically when she pulled out of it to stare at him long and hard. She loved him so much it hurt. It hurt especially to see the sooty evidence of just how dangerous it could be fighting fires for a living.

She might have thought it terribly sexy and exciting at nineteen but just thinking about what might have happened today had that ceiling fallen on him, or what could happen to him in the future, sucked her breath away. "You scared me half to death tonight," she said, sitting back again, searching his gaze.

"I'm fine."

Arabella shook her head. "You have a dislocated shoulder and a ceiling almost fell on your head."

"But it didn't."

"But what if it had?"

"I was wearing a helmet. Plus I have a very hard head."

He was making light of it but she didn't see anything funny about it. "Your job is dangerous."

"Yes." He nodded. "If you're untrained and you don't know what you're doing. But I *am* trained and I *do* know what I'm doing and my safety and that of the guys I work with is paramount. I'm good at my job, Bella."

His fingers stroked lazy patterns from her hip to her buttocks and she fought the urge to close her eyes. He was *good* at that too. The sensation tingled between her legs where his dick lay taut and hard and she rocked against it involuntarily.

"That doesn't mean I'm not going to worry about you every time I hear a bloody siren."

His fingers stopped their maddening pattern, his eyes opened, burning bright, piercing her with their intensity.

"No," he said, shaking his head. "You've told me, quite rightly, that I'm going to have to live with the fact that your memory is never going to come back. Well, Bella, you're going to have to live with the fact that *occasionally* my job can be dangerous but that I take my safety very seriously and I promise you I will *always* come home to you. *Always.*"

Arabella knew that no one in life could make that kind of

promise but conviction blazed like lightning in his eyes. She'd asked something impossible of him, she'd asked him to give up hope and now he was asking something just as hard of her.

She'd only known him for a few months but she already knew being a firefighter was as much a part of Logan as the air he breathed and he was asking her to put her trust and faith in his abilities.

How could she not after all they'd been through together?

She swallowed. "Okay."

He shook his head, eyes still blazing. "Tell me you believe me. Tell me you know that I'll always come home to you."

"I believe you." And she did.

His abdominal muscles tensed as he curled up, his mouth claiming hers in a hard, greedy kiss, his tongue demanding entry. They fell back into the water together and Arabella froze as his shoulder was jostled and he grunted.

A hot spike of concern dragged her off him. "Shit, are you okay?"

He didn't bother to answer her, his mouth a grim line as his gaze dropped to her breasts before returning to her face again. He thrust the loofah at her. "Finish what you started so I can get out of this filthy bath and love you properly."

"But your shoulder," Arabella protested.

"Screw my shoulder."

A wave of dizzy need clenched Arabella's abdominal muscles tight. He looked pretty damn serious. And she was sure they could figure it out. She reached for the soap.

"Marry me."

She blinked, her heart practically stopping in her chest. "*What?*"

"I love you, Bella. And this is exactly where I belong. With you. Forever."

Arabella's chest expanded. It sounded so simple but nothing had ever felt so right. "Yes."

Because she was exactly where she belonged. With him. Forever.

The End

The Hot Aussie Knights

Headed by grandfather Leonard (The Legend) Knight, the Knight family is fire-fighting royalty in Australia. Two generations have followed in Leonard's highly distinguished footsteps and nowadays, despite being scattered across the length and breadth of Australia, it's the five Knight cousins who keep the Hot Aussie Knight legacy alive, working hard and playing hard, day and night.

Book 1: *Hot Mess* by Amy Andrews

Book 2: *Burning Both Ends* by Sinclair Jayne

Book 3: *Long Hot Summer* by Victoria Purman

Book 4: *Burning Love* by Trish Morey

Available now at your favorite online retailer!

About the Author

Multi-award winning and USA Today bestselling author **Amy Andrews** is an Aussie who has written fifty romances from novellas to category to single-title in both the traditional and digital markets for a variety of publishers. Her first love is steamy contemporary romance that makes her readers tingle, laugh and sigh. At the age of 16, she met a guy she instantly knew she was going to marry. She just smiles when people tell her insta-love books are unrealistic because she did marry that man and, twenty odd years later, they're still living out their happily ever after. Amy works part-time as a PICU nurse and spent six years on the national executive of Romance Writers of Australia where she organized two national conferences and undertook a two year term as president. She loves good books, fab food, great wine and frequent travel – preferably all four together. She lives on acreage on the outskirts of Brisbane with a gorgeous mountain view but secretly wishes it was the hillsides of Tuscany.

Visit her website at AmyAndrews.com.au

Thank you for reading

Hot Mess

If you enjoyed this book, you can find more from all our great authors at TulePublishing.com, or from your favorite online retailer.

TULE
PUBLISHING

Printed in Great Britain
by Amazon

35156357R00147